THE DOG'S
MEOW

THE DOG'S MEOW

MICHELLE SCHUSTERMAN

Scholastic Inc.

10 9 8 7 6 5 4 3   21 22 23 24 25

Printed in the U.S.A.   40
First printing 2021

Book design by Keirsten Geise

For Jake and Rosa

THE DOG'S MEOW

Chapter One

Mina

A cool breeze rippled the white tents, and Mina shivered. Not just from the almost-fall chill in the air, but from excitement. Sure, she'd been coming to the farmers' market in downtown Fairbanks every weekend since before she could walk. Her dad's tourism business, Golden Heart Dogsledding Excursions, attracted lots of travelers looking for a real Alaskan adventure. And the farmers' market was just as popular with locals—everyone came out, especially when the weather was nice.

But today was exciting for another reason.

"Ready, Mina?" Dad asked. He was standing behind a table covered in pamphlets and photos of huskies. Mina's mom was a professional dog breeder, and the picture of their newest litter of fuzzy gray pups with curious blue eyes and lolling pink tongues was featured in the center of the table. Kodiak and Suka, two of Dad's current sled dog team members, flanked him on either side, ready to greet anyone who stopped by the tent.

"I'm ready," Mina said eagerly. Niko, the team's lead dog, nuzzled her hand encouragingly. For what felt like the hundredth time, Mina checked her setup: a rack with six T-shirts, each displaying a different design, a box with another twenty-four folded shirts, and a sign that read:

CLOCKWORK T-SHIRTS BY
MINA'S ORIGINAL DESIGNS
ONLY $10 EACH!

ClockWork was Mina's favorite band. Actually, that was a huge understatement. ClockWork was Mina's reason for *living.* (Well, maybe that was a little overdramatic.) There were six members, each one with their own distinct look and vocal style, and Mina could sing along with any of their harmonies on every single track of their debut album, *Borrowed*. She also knew each of their favorite foods, animals, colors, and inspirational quotes, thanks to the interviews she'd managed to find online. The personalities and unique characteristics of the members had been the inspiration for her T-shirt designs.

Mina had spent most of her summer break working on her business plan, with lots of help from Dad. She'd bought the art and silk-screening supplies with her allowance money and hand printed all thirty shirts. At ten dollars each, she only needed to sell eight shirts to break even. And if she sold out completely, she'd make $220 in profit!

"Logan! Mina!"

Niko's ears perked up, and her tail began to wag. Mina and Dad both turned to see Hope Wakefield ducking under the tent next to theirs, carrying a giant cooler with the words HOPE'S FIREWEED HONEY stenciled on the front.

"Hi, Ms. Wakefield!" Mina called back. "Need any help setting up?"

"Nah, but thanks, sweetie." Ms. Wakefield blew a stray strand of graying blond hair out of her eyes as she set the cooler on the ground. Straightening up, she winked at Mina. "Although I may need help finishing off these samples by the end of the day. I'm debuting a new flavor—star thistle!"

"Ooh, *yum*," Mina said emphatically. "Did you bring any wildflower honey truffles?"

"Of course!" Ms. Wakefield glanced at Niko, who gazed back at her eagerly, and she laughed. "Yes, Niko, I brought peanut butter honey treats, too."

Niko yipped appreciatively as Ms. Wakefield began unpacking bottles of honey from the cooler. Ms. Wakefield's eyes flicked over to the rack of T-shirts, and she shot Dad a questioning look. "New merch, Logan?"

"Actually, you're looking at the debut of Mina's Original Designs," Dad replied, and Mina felt herself flush with pride—and a fresh wave of anxiety.

Ms. Wakefield's eyes widened. "Is that so?

An entrepreneur at age twelve, eh?" Smiling, she walked over, still holding a few bottles of buckwheat honey.

"I made them all by hand," Mina said, stepping to the side and gesturing to her display. Every time she looked at her fun, colorful designs, she felt like she might burst with pride.

"My goodness," Ms. Wakefield said. "These are impressive! And what is ClockWork, exactly?"

"A band," Mina said immediately. "There are six members, so I designed a shirt for each member, based on their personalities and stuff. See how the clock hands on this one are actually tiny chili peppers? That's because Lyric loves spicy food. Oh, and this one, see how the numbers run counterclockwise? That's because River is the only member who's left-handed! And Gentry is obsessed with scary movies, so this one has—"

"Mina, hon," Dad interrupted gently. "I'm sure Ms. Wakefield wants to finish getting her booth set up."

Mina looked up at Ms. Wakefield, whose smile

had become rather fixed. "Oh! Yeah, of course," Mina said sheepishly.

Niko gave her hand a quick lick, and Mina scratched her behind the ears. Sometimes she thought the husky was the only other person—er, dog—who really *got* ClockWork. When Mina played "Time to Make You Mine" in her room, turning her computer speakers to top volume, Niko would roll over on her back and squirm happily on the carpet. And when "Every Second Counts" reached the chorus, Niko would tilt her head back and howl, her mouth a perfectly round O.

Earlier that summer, ClockWork had announced that they were going on their first international tour. Of course, Fairbanks wasn't one of the stops. The closest one was Seattle, and that was a four-hour flight away! Mina knew she didn't have a chance of seeing ClockWork live. But suddenly, just listening to their songs didn't feel like enough anymore. That was when inspiration had struck, and Mina's Original Designs was born.

As Ms. Wakefield went back to unpacking her

cooler, Dad turned to Mina with a smile. "Do you have that receipt book?"

Mina patted the purple fanny pack around her waist. "Receipts, two pens, and change in tens, fives, and ones," she recited.

"Let me know if you need any help," Dad said, planting a kiss on the top of her head. "Good luck, hon!"

"Thanks!"

Mina took a deep breath and faced the front of the tent. A few early birds were already at Mr. Waska's Wildlife Photography tent, admiring the massive framed image of a moose bull staring right at the camera, delicately holding a pine cone between its teeth. On the other side of Dad's tent, Jeannie and Lisa Wilson-Gray chatted amiably with a small group of tourists, who ended up buying several of their hand-carved birch bark bowls to ship back home to Boston.

Mina watched them, one hand mindlessly toying with Niko's soft, pointy ears. She hadn't even thought about shipping! Then again, it was probably a lot easier to pack a souvenir T-shirt in your suit-case than a souvenir wooden punch bowl.

As usual, Dad's tent was popular with the tour-ists. Of course, that was mostly due to Niko, Kodiak, and Suka, who had a little routine that always did the trick when things slowed down. First, Suka would wander away from their booth and trot up and down the path between the tents. An almost purely snow-white husky, Suka never had a problem getting people's attention. When someone stopped to greet her, she'd give their hand a quick sniff, allow them to pat her head once or twice, then trot back into Dad's tent. The tourists would usually follow, then burst out laughing at the sight of Kodiak, a seventy-five-pound ball of black-and-tan fur, lying flat on his back and waiting for his belly rub. As the tourists indulged Kodiak, Niko would emerge from behind the table carrying a Golden Heart Dogsledding Excursions pamphlet between her teeth, which she would pre-sent to the tourists. They always found the whole thing utterly charming, and everyone left with a pamphlet and a smile on their face.

Not everyone signed up for an excursion, of course. But business was pretty good, and Dad always said it was because Niko, Kodiak, and Suka were the best salespeople—er, sales*dogs*—in all Alaska.

By two o'clock, Mina was wondering if the huskies would be better at selling T-shirts than she was, too.

Nearly every single tourist who stopped by Dad's tent noticed Mina's Original Designs. Several had come over to take a closer look at the shirts, and three had even complimented them and asked Mina about her designs.

But no one had heard of ClockWork. And Mina hadn't sold a single shirt.

"Hey, Trooper Jack!"

Mina glanced up as Dad stood to greet the tall, lanky man who'd just entered their tent. Trooper Jack grinned as he shook Dad's hand, then knelt down to rub Kodiak's belly.

"How's my favorite rescue team?" he asked. Kodiak let out a happy whine as he squirmed, making Mina giggle.

"They're too full of peanut butter honey treats to rescue anyone right now," she said, and Trooper Jack chuckled.

Dad was studying his clipboard, frowning slightly. "That's strange. I usually have twice this many folks signed up for tours by this time."

Trooper Jack sighed as he got to his feet. "Tourism's been pretty sluggish since summer ended. It's mostly locals here today."

"We need that first real snow to come in!" Dad said with a sigh. "So how's everything with you, Jack?"

Mina glanced at her unsold T-shirts as the two men fell into conversation. Snow was good for Dad's business, but it probably wouldn't make a difference in her sales. Dad must have noticed her dejected expression, because he suddenly tossed down his clipboard.

"How about a kettle corn break?" he suggested in an overly cheerful tone. "Or maybe some of Nancy's double dark fudge?"

Mina tucked a lock of dark hair behind her ear

and tried to smile. "No, thanks. I'm still full from lunch."

That wasn't entirely true. Mina had only been able to eat half the ham sandwich she'd brought. Although she *had* managed to eat three of Ms. Wakefield's honey truffles.

"Well, I definitely need some kettle corn," Trooper Jack said.

"Same here," Dad agreed. "Mina, you don't mind watching the booth for a few minutes?"

"Sure!"

"Thanks, hon." Dad smiled at her. "I'll bring back some kettle corn, in case you change your mind."

Mina watched as Dad and Trooper Jack disappeared into the crowd. Usually, she loved talking to people who stopped by the tent and answering their questions about breeding huskies, dogsledding races, and even the occasional rescue mission. Her favorite story to tell tourists was the one about how Trooper Jack had come to Dad for help when a couple had gotten lost on a hike two summers ago. Mina, Dad, and the huskies had raced into the wilderness, searching for nearly two hours before finding them. The couple actually hadn't been that far off the path, but they hadn't had any supplies on them and weren't dressed appropriately for the cold, so they'd been really scared. Telling that story made Mina feel like a hero.

But right now, she couldn't muster any enthusiasm. Not when her own business was starting to look like a total failure.

Suddenly, Niko sat up straight, tail wagging furiously. Mina followed the husky's gaze to a familiar blond head, and she felt her stomach sink into her shoes.

Emily Cooper stood just a few tents away, her freckled face lit up with laughter. As the crowd thinned, Mina saw who Emily was talking to, and she groaned.

"The F Twins," she whispered to Niko, who tilted her head curiously. Faith Nelson and Fiona Mitchell were two of the most popular girls in Mina's class. They'd all be starting seventh grade on Monday. The F Twins had been best friends all through elementary school, just like Mina and Emily. But for some reason, they'd invited Emily to the movies with them a week into summer break. Mina hadn't been too worried at first, just confused—and maybe a little bit hurt. When the F Twins had brought Emily to a barbecue at the Mitchells' house a few days later, Mina told herself it was just a weird phase.

But if it was a phase, it was a really long one. And it still wasn't over. Mina and Emily hadn't had a fight or anything like that, but Mina had barely seen her best friend all summer. If Emily even considered her a best friend anymore.

"Please don't come over, please don't come over," Mina murmured under her breath, turning away slightly and casting quick, furtive glances at the three girls.

Niko's tail wagged even harder, and Mina realized what was about to happen a split second too late.

"Woof!"

The single, commanding bark caused dozens of heads to turn in their direction. Including Emily's. Her eyes met Mina's, and she froze.

A strange mix of joy and dread flooded through Mina. Tentatively, she raised her hand and waved. After a second, Emily smiled and waved back.

Heart pounding, Mina watched as Emily said something to the F Twins. Then the three of them started walking toward Mina's tent. Niko bounded out to greet Emily, and Suka and Kodiak quickly followed suit. Emily giggled as they swarmed her, vying for ear scratches and belly rubs.

"Aw, I've missed you guys," she said, kneeling down to hug them. Mina wanted to say, *What about me? Did you miss me, too?*

But instead, she just said, "Hey, Emily." Super casual, as if she hadn't spent the whole summer wondering why her best friend never seemed to want to hang out with her.

"Hi, Mina." Emily didn't stand, but she grinned up at Mina. Was it Mina's imagination, or did she look a little guilty?

"What's up, Mina?" Fiona said, flipping her long red braid over her shoulder.

Next to her, Faith smiled at Mina. "Your dogs are awesome."

"Yeah, they are," Mina agreed. The F Twins sounded friendly enough, but Mina still felt on edge. If they liked her—really, genuinely *liked* her—they wouldn't have stolen her best friend. They would have invited Mina to hang out with them, too. But they were clearly a trio now, and Mina was the odd one out.

"Hey, what's that?" Fiona pointed, and Mina stepped aside so they could see the sign over the rack of T-shirts. When other visitors had stopped to look at her shirts, Mina had felt proud. But now she experienced an odd twinge deep in her belly. Like maybe she should have moved to block the sign from their view instead.

"Oh, wow, did you *make* these?" Faith's dark brown eyes lit up momentarily. But as her gaze moved from shirt to shirt, her expression changed. It was a really subtle change, but Mina noticed it. Her lips quirked up just enough to make her smile a smirk, and she shot Fiona a pointed look.

"Ah. ClockWork." Fiona stifled a giggle, and Mina felt her face grow hot.

"Yeah, I made them," she said, unsure why she suddenly felt defensive. "I created a design for each member. See? Gentry, Lyric, River, Sage, Zion, Halo." She pointed to each shirt in turn, then shot a hopeful look at Emily.

Mina and Emily had discovered ClockWork together last winter. They'd spent hours and hours sprawled on the beanbag chairs in Mina's room, reading to each other the juiciest tidbits from the band members' interviews, singing along to their songs at the top of their lungs. If anyone in Fairbanks could appreciate the details Mina had put into these designs, it was Emily.

But the smile on Emily's face wasn't quite right. In fact, Mina realized with a pang, it looked forced, kind of like Ms. Wakefield's smile had been.

"That's so cool!" Emily said, even though she'd barely glanced at the shirts. "Seriously, Mina. It's amazing that you started your own business. How many have you sold?"

Mina swallowed. "Um, well, just a few so far." Her voice had gone all high, and she was positive the others could tell she was lying. "Anyway, it was good to see you guys! I should, um, get back to work."

She waved, then headed behind the table, with the huskies obediently trotting after her. Mina busied herself rearranging Dad's pamphlets and looking through his binder, pretending she had some important task to take care of. Her face felt like it was on fire despite the chilly air, and when she glanced up after a minute, Emily and the F Twins were several tents away.

Exhaling shakily, Mina sank down into a folding chair. Niko sat at her side, her cold nose nudging Mina's hand.

No best friend, and her business was a total bust. *Well*, Mina thought bracingly. *At least today can't get any worse.*

Chapter Two

Niko

After a while, Niko joined Dad as he helped a man from California sign up for an excursion. But she kept a watchful eye on Mina, who sat slumped in a folding chair next to her T-shirts, her expression glum. She was upset, and Niko knew why.

Lifting her snout, Niko sniffed the air carefully. Emily's scent—a mix of citrus and pine trees—still lingered. Niko peered around the tourist Dad was talking to and scanned the faces in the crowd.

Suka appeared at her side, nudging her gently and glancing pointedly in the opposite direction. "She's over there."

Niko turned and, after a moment, spotted Emily with those two girls again. They were sharing a sleeve of kettle corn—Niko's second-favorite market treat after Ms. Wakefield's peanut butter honey snacks—and giggling over something on Emily's phone.

Exhaling softly, Niko turned away. But Suka was still watching Emily, her eyes narrowed, the hairs on her back standing up slightly.

"Traitor." Suka sniffed disapprovingly. "How could she leave Mina for another pack?"

Niko wanted to defend Emily. After all, she'd known Emily since she was just a pup—all the dogs in Niko's pack had grown up playing with Mina and Emily. They'd all noticed Emily's absence over the summer. And Niko had definitely noticed the change in Mina's mood. But she'd been hoping Emily had been away with her family, like two years ago, when the Coopers had spent almost a month in Texas visiting Emily's grandmother. Mina had been sad then, too.

But this was a different kind of sad, and Niko didn't like the smell of it.

Behind them, Kodiak gnawed noisily on a giant

rawhide bone. He paused to glance over at Emily, too, his ears flattening against his head. "She's not a traitor. Humans are different, Suka."

Suka snorted. "I know that. But look." She jerked her head in Mina's direction. Kodiak and Niko turned, and Niko felt a tug in her chest when she realized Mina was watching Emily as well. Suka let out another huffy breath. "That's betrayal. Mina and Emily were a pack, just like us."

Kodiak didn't respond. After a moment, he went back to chewing his bone, though with much less gusto. Niko looked back at Suka, arching her brows. "Maybe you're right. But there's nothing we can do."

"That's what you think."

Niko recognized the glint in Suka's light blue eyes a second too late. She let out a sharp bark— "Suka, no!"—but the slender white husky was already bounding out of the tent, heading straight for Emily.

"Suka!" Dad cried, surprised. Mina half stood out of her chair, her expression quickly changing from alarmed to confused to mortified as she realized what was happening. Tail wagging, Suka leaped up and placed her two front paws on Emily's chest. Emily burst into giggles and said something Niko couldn't hear as she scratched Suka behind the ears. Then Suka fell gracefully onto all four paws again, gently gripped the sleeve of Emily's hoodie, and began tugging her toward the tent.

Toward Mina.

Emily was still laughing, but it was a different kind of laugh now, forced and awkward. As Mina's face went bright red, Niko decided enough was enough. She slipped past Dad and the tourists, who seemed to be enjoying the whole spectacle, and trotted to the front of the tent before letting out two short barks.

"Suka! Stop!"

Suka was probably the most independent dog in their pack. That quality made her an excellent swing dog. Her position on the gangline was right behind Niko, and when Niko would make a turn, Suka would resist the urge to follow and instead swing wider, helping to guide the rest of the team into an arc and ensure everyone made it safely around the corner.

But not even stubborn Suka could ignore such a sharp command from the leader of the pack. She released Emily's sleeve and, with obvious reluctance, ambled back over to the tent.

"Sorry about that, Emily!" Dad called, and Mina let out a soft groan.

Emily still had that strange, tight smile on her face. "No problem!" she replied, casting a quick glance at Mina before turning back to her snickering friends. Niko watched as Mina buried her face in her hands, and she shot Suka a sharp look.

"You made things worse!" Niko snapped.

Suka curled up next to Kodiak and began diligently cleaning her paws. "Someone had to try to bring Emily back."

Niko sighed. "Kodiak was right—humans aren't huskies, Suka. Emily isn't a stray who wandered off and got lost." If anything, Niko realized, Mina was the one who looked like an abandoned pup, with her slumped shoulders and downcast eyes.

Dad noticed the change in Mina's behavior, too. He didn't say anything, but Niko saw him glance at her in concern every few minutes. Every time someone stopped to admire Mina's shirts, Mina would perk up a little. But then they'd walk away empty-handed, and she'd slide even lower in her chair. By the time the farmers' market began to close up, Mina looked ready to curl up on the ground next to a loudly snoring Kodiak.

Niko watched sadly as Mina took the six T-shirts off the rack, folded them, and packed them in the box with the others. She tossed the bag that had been strapped around her waist on top of the shirts, then closed the box.

"Well, that was a pretty slow day," Ms. Wakefield said, packing up her cooler. "Although at least I sold out of the star thistle. How'd you do, sweetie?"

Mina's voice sounded oddly thick. "Well, not too good."

Dad was at her side immediately with a supportive hand on her shoulder. "Which is absolutely normal for a brand-new business. Isn't that right, Hope?"

Ms. Wakefield's expression changed when she saw Mina's face. "Oh—yes, very much so! You won't remember this, Mina, but you were here the first day I tried selling my honey at the market. That was, what, eight years ago, Logan?"

"Sounds about right," Dad said, nodding encouragingly.

"Didn't sell a single bottle," Ms. Wakefield went on. "But I did hand out nearly six bottles' worth of free samples. At least you broke even!"

Niko saw Mina force a smile. "Yeah, handing out free shirt samples would've been a bad business move."

That got a laugh from Dad and Ms. Wakefield, and Mina seemed slightly cheered. Niko sat with Suka and a still-snoring Kodiak while Dad and Mina loaded all their supplies into Dad's pickup truck. When Dad whistled, Niko gave Kodiak's ear a gentle nip to wake him up. He yawned widely as he stood, giving himself a good shake before following Niko and Suka. Mina held the passenger door open, and they clambered in one at a time—Niko

24

first, followed by Suka, then Kodiak. Once they were all in the back, Mina slid her seat back and climbed in as Dad started the truck. Niko poked her head between the front seats and gave Mina a quick kiss on the cheek, and she giggled.

"Thanks," she whispered, snuggling Niko's face. "I needed that."

Dad rolled the windows down before pulling out of the parking lot. Kodiak was already snoring again, and Suka was working at a small knot of fur on her tail with her teeth. Niko pressed herself against the window and stuck her head out, enjoying the cold breeze and all the interesting scents it carried. The drive home was her favorite part of market day. Dad always took the same route, a long and winding road through the forest, and the wind held all sorts of stories for Niko's nose to decipher: the earthy scent of a family of brown bears on the move a few miles away; the oddly sweet aroma that meant the trees would be shedding their dried-up leaves soon; the rubbery, burning smell that happened when a car screeched to a halt—to avoid hitting a deer, Niko realized, catching the scent of the animal's fear and confusion still lingering in the air.

Suddenly, one of Niko's very favorite smells filled her nostrils: the fresh, pure smell that could only mean one thing.

Snow.

Niko wriggled ecstatically, sticking her head farther out the window. And sure enough, the tiny, white flakes began to fall.

"Hey, first snow of the year!" Dad said, and Niko wagged her tail in response.

Mina giggled. "I think someone's excited."

Niko's tail wagged even harder. Snow meant winter. And winter meant *racing.* Leading her team and Dad through the wilderness, tearing across the endless trails that passed over hills and through the mountains, breathing in the frigid air and having the time of her life. There was nothing Niko loved more than sled racing.

Mina twisted around in her seat. "What about you, Suka? Are you excited about the snow?" Suka abandoned her grooming and sat up, tail thump-thump-thumping against her seat. "Kodiak, what do you think?"

Kodiak's response was an extra-loud snore, which made Mina giggle. But Niko didn't notice. Her entire body had just gone rigid. Something was wrong—she'd caught a whiff of it, just for a split second. Niko leaned farther out the window, paws hanging outside, and took a good, long sniff.

There it was again! It was similar to the smell of the deer, confused and afraid. But that had been sharper, more urgent. This new scent was a slower, sleepier sort of confused. Niko had never smelled anything quite like it before, and it made all her fur stand on end.

Someone needed help. *Now.*

Chapter Three

NUKKA

RRRROOOOOOAAAARRRR!

The creature stirred slightly at the sound but didn't open her eyes. She was curled into a tight ball, tucked away under a brambly bush. Sometimes, when she was in an especially deep sleep, vague memories played in her mind: other warm, wriggling bodies; a rough, pink tongue cleaning her; the delicious taste of milk; and the full belly she always had after feeding.

At least, she was pretty sure those were memories. But maybe they were just dreams.

For all the creature knew, she'd been alone under this bush her whole, short life. She was totally numb to the cold now. She didn't even shiver much anymore. That was a good thing. Right?

Deep inside, she knew the answer. *No, it's not. It's not a good thing at all.*

Something light landed on the creature's nose and stayed there. Mustering all her strength, she stuck the tip of her tongue out and caught it—a delicate, tiny thing that melted in her mouth in a pleasant way. Blearily, the creature blinked her eyes open.

Other than the shift from dark to light and back to dark again, her surroundings never changed. There were trees and grass and bushes, and a long, black path for the occasional beast to zoom down with a ROAR.

But now tiny white bits of fluff were falling from the sky. They whirled and twirled in the air, spinning around and around before coming to rest on the ground, the trees, even the brambles of the bush. The creature watched, enchanted, as these bits of fluff slowly turned the world from green to white.

RRRROOOOOOAAAARRRR!

Another beast zoomed past, making the creature dizzy with its speed. They were so quick, she was never able to get a good look at them. While they were all huge, some were much bigger than others. Some were kind of rectangular, others more round. The only thing they all seemed to have in common was that when it was dark outside, their eyes glowed a yellow so bright that the creature could see nothing but dancing lights long after they were gone.

She'd been afraid of them, at first. But they never seemed to notice her, and they never stopped.

The bits of white fluff were sticking to her fur. She caught a few more on her tongue, enjoying the feel of them melting down her throat. The ground beneath her rumbled slightly, and she braced herself for another beast.

RRRROOOOOOAAAARRRR!

It flew past, just like all the others. But then, something different happened. The beast slowed down... and stopped. Instead of roaring, it made a softer noise, one that was almost familiar, like... like...

Purrrrrr.

The creature felt a strange tug in her chest. She wanted to lift her head and look at the beast, but she was too weak. The soft rumble was growing closer and closer. Was the beast coming back? She'd never heard one move so quietly before.

The movement stopped, and the purring abruptly ended. For a moment, the air was absolutely still and quiet. Then the creature heard a new sound, one she'd definitely never heard before. A sharp, urgent sound.

"Arf!"

Chapter Four

Mina

"Niko!"

Mina twisted all the way around in her seat, stretching her arms out toward Niko. But the gray-and-white husky was struggling to fit through the half-open window.

"Dad!" Mina cried, her heart hammering wildly. "She's trying to jump out!"

Dad's mouth was a thin line as he slowly backed the truck up to the spot they'd passed when Niko had begun frantically pawing at the window. Suka stood still in the middle seat, her snout high as she sniffed intently. Even Kodiak was alert, the black fur around his neck sticking out straight like a short lion's mane.

The moment Dad put the truck in park, Mina unclasped her seat belt and lunged for Niko. But the husky just wriggled out of her grasp and began barking, the sound like an ear-splitting siren.

"Arf-arf-arf-arf-arf!"

Grimacing, Dad hopped out of the truck and started to move his seat forward. "Whoa, girl!" he exclaimed, jumping back as Niko launched herself over the console and leaped out of the truck.

"Dad, what's she doing?" Mina scrambled out of the driver's side, and Dad closed the door quickly.

"Stay," he commanded Suka and Kodiak through the half-open window. Suka whined lightly, but neither husky moved as Dad and Mina jogged after Niko.

The sun had already set, and the dim light combined with the fresh snow made everything a dreamy blue-gray color. Mina knew that dusk was one of the most dangerous times of day for visibility, even worse than when it was totally dark outside.

But Mina also knew that visibility didn't matter

as much if you had a husky's sense of smell. It was practically a superpower.

And Niko obviously smelled something. Or maybe—Mina's stomach flipped at the thought—some*one*. The few times Mina had accompanied Dad and Niko on rescue missions, Niko had moved fast once she closed in on the smell of the lost party. But Mina had never seen Niko this frantic. It was frightening. What if whoever or whatever she smelled was really badly hurt? Or worse?

Mina grabbed Dad's hand, and he squeezed it tightly as they slowed to a walk, their shoes crunching on the thin layer of fresh snow. Niko was darting around a cluster of thimbleberry bushes, sniffing frantically, her tail sticking straight out. She froze, then shoved her head under the bush, showering the grass with snow flurries.

"There can't be anyone under there," Mina said, frowning. "Even a little kid couldn't fit."

"Hmm" was all Dad said. He knelt down next to Niko, who immediately emerged from the bush and gave his face a quick lick. As Mina joined them, Dad peered under the bush. Then he pulled his phone from his pocket, flipped on the flashlight, and lifted the bottom leaves a little higher. For a moment, Mina didn't understand what she was looking at. Then she gasped.

Curled up under the bush was the tiniest creature she'd ever seen, even smaller than Nanuk, the littlest pup in Sakari's current litter. And unlike those healthy, pink-bellied pups, this creature was scrawny, its fur so matted with dirt and snow that Mina couldn't even tell what color it was. For a terrible second, Mina thought it might not be breathing. Then its eyes fluttered open, and it let out a high, pitiful sound.

"Mew!"

"It's a kitten!" Mina cried, reaching for it instinctively. But Dad placed his hand on her arm.

"Don't touch it yet," he said, and his voice was calm and controlled, like it was on every rescue mission. "There's a blanket under the driver's seat in the truck."

"Okay," Mina whispered, tearing her gaze from the pitiful kitten. "Be right back."

She sprinted back to the truck, where two pairs of crystal-blue eyes stared at her intently from the window. Mina threw open the door and stuck her hand under the seat, feeling for the blanket. Her fingers grasped the soft cotton fleece, and she yanked the blanket free.

"Stay there," Mina called to Suka and Kodiak, already slamming the door closed. She ran back toward Dad and Niko, clutching the blanket to her chest.

"Thanks, sweetie." Dad took the blanket as Mina fell to her knees, panting. She watched nervously as he unfolded it in his palms, then gently slid his hands under the bush and scooped up the kitten. The tiny creature barely stirred, and Mina felt tears stinging behind her eyes.

"Are we taking it home?" she asked, her voice shaking.

Carefully, Dad wrapped the kitten up so that only its face poked out of the swaddle. "I think we'd better take it straight to Dr. Li," he replied.

Mina nodded. Dr. Li was the huskies'

veterinarian. She would know just what to do to help the poor kitten.

Niko stuck close to Mina's side as she followed Dad back to the truck. No one spoke as they all climbed inside, and Suka and Kodiak peered curiously at the bundle in Dad's arms. Once Mina was buckled in, Dad held out the bundle. Mina took it, her hands trembling slightly, and cradled the kitten in her lap. Niko leaned over the seat and rested her head on Mina's shoulder, both of them staring at the kitten's tiny face. Two glassy amber eyes gazed up at them. Mina felt a hot lump forming in her throat as Dad started the engine and flipped on the headlights.

"The kitten's going to be okay, right?"

Dad checked the rearview mirror before guiding the truck back onto the road and swinging it around in a wide U-turn.

"We'll do everything we can," he replied.

Which wasn't the answer Mina wanted to hear. It wasn't really an answer at all.

She couldn't believe that just a few minutes ago,

her mind had been filled with thoughts of the box of unsold T-shirts in the back of the truck and the expression on Emily's face when Suka had tried to drag her back over to Mina. Emily had looked so embarrassed, but not nearly as embarrassed as Mina had felt. She'd spent most of the drive staring out the window, worrying about seeing Emily at school on Monday, wondering if the F Twins would tell everyone about how no one had bought a single ClockWork shirt.

All of that suddenly seemed to matter a lot less.

Niko let out a soft whimper that Mina under-stood completely. She hugged the bundled kitten close as the truck sped down the road, heading back to Fairbanks.

Chapter Five

Niko

Niko normally loved visiting the vet. Dr. Li was kind and gentle, and she always had a giant jar full of treats in her office. Most of the times Niko came to see Dr. Li, it was just for a checkup. The few times she'd been here because she was sick, Dr. Li had made her feel better the moment she appeared. The vet had a special kind of energy—calm yet commanding—that soothed Niko.

But as Dr. Li examined the scrawny little kitten, Niko couldn't help thinking she'd never seen the vet look so grim. Not even when Kodiak had swallowed a whole entire ear of corn and Dr. Li had had to do not one but *two* complicated procedures to get it out.

"Hmm," Dr. Li murmured as she took the kitten's temperature. "Hmm."

"I don't understand how she ended up under that bush," Mina said, her voice more high-pitched than usual. She was perched on the edge of the chair closest to Dr. Li's examination table, her hand gripping Niko's fur for support. Niko could practically feel Mina's anxiety, and her muscles tightened in response.

"She might have been abandoned," Dad said quietly. "Or maybe she just strayed from the litter, wandered off. It happens." Niko saw him glance through the window in the door, and she knew he was checking to make sure Suka and Kodiak were still with the receptionist.

Dr. Li straightened up. "I'm going to take her to the back to run a few tests. Would you like to wait here?"

Dad nodded, sinking down into the chair next to Mina's. "Thanks, Carol."

"Be right back." Dr. Li kept her tone light as she gently wrapped the kitten in a soft blanket, but

Niko could hear the worry in her voice. Niko gazed at the kitten as Dr. Li carried her out of the office and down the hall.

Suddenly, Mina let out a loud sniffle. Niko looked up to see a tear trickle down her cheek, and she nuzzled Mina's hand with her nose.

"It's going to be okay, hon," Dad said, slipping his arm around Mina and giving her a squeeze. "Don't worry."

Mina nodded miserably. Niko thought about the look on her face as she'd packed up her T-shirts while the farmers' market closed down, and when Emily had resisted Suka's attempts to lead her back to Mina. She'd been sad then. Now she looked positively devastated.

The three of them waited in silence for what felt like hours before Dr. Li returned. Mina shot to her feet, her face filled with hope. But Niko knew the moment she saw Dr. Li's expression that despite what Dad had said, things might *not* be okay.

"I'm still running a few tests, but she doesn't appear to have any infections," Dr. Li said, resting her hands on the examination table. "However, she's severely dehydrated and malnourished."

"So she just needs food and water, and she'll get better?" Mina asked hopefully.

Dr. Li smiled, but her eyes were filled with sympathy. "We have a special milk formula just for kittens, yes. But she's very young—only a few weeks old at the most. Those early days are vital for kittens."

"Just like for pups," Dad said, placing a comforting hand on Mina's back. "Remember when Sakari's litter was born, how we had to bottle-feed Nanuk every few hours when he wasn't eating on his own?"

"And this kitten has been without water or her mother's milk for days," Dr. Li added. "We'll do everything we can to help her. But..." She paused, glancing at Dad, and Niko stiffened. "But there's a good chance we won't be able to save her."

Mina stifled a sob. "Is there anything we can do to help?" she asked, wiping her eyes. "Can we see her?"

"Of course," Dr. Li replied immediately. "Just as soon as my team is finished running tests, we'll bring her back in here. I'm sure having all of you close by will help comfort her." She gave them one last small smile, then hurried out of the office.

Dad turned to face Mina. "You okay?" he asked softly.

She nodded. "Yeah."

"Good." Dad scratched Niko behind the ears. "I'm going to check on Suka and Kodiak, then give Mom a call and let her know what's going on. Be right back."

As soon as he left, Mina sat down heavily in her chair. Niko stood and moved to stand in front of her, resting her head on Mina's knees. Mina's eyes were closed, and she took several long, deep breaths. When she opened her eyes and met Niko's gaze, Niko saw the same fierce determination she was feeling. She and Mina were thinking the same thing.

This kitten was not going to die if they could help it.

Chapter Six

NUKKA

The creature slept for a long, long time.

She was warm and her belly was full. Sometimes she heard voices nearby, and that was usually followed by someone gently poking and prodding her. She could smell the clean, soapy scent of their skin, and after a while, she felt comforted by the familiarity of the scent. But she was far too sleepy to bother opening her eyes to see what they looked like.

Then, after hours and hours of blissful sleep, the creature heard another voice. It was higher and younger than the others. Her skin had a different scent, too—fresh and warm and a little bit sweet, like milk. The visitor moved closer to the creature, and after a moment, another scent reached the creature's nose. A familiar scent that got her attention right away.

Fur.

The creature's curiosity overcame her sleepiness, at least for a few seconds. Mustering all her strength, she opened her eyes and peered at her visitor. She saw a young girl with black hair pulled away from her round, pink-cheeked face. The girl's eyes were greenish gold, and they went wide with surprise when the creature blinked.

"Niko, look!" the girl exclaimed. "She's awake!"

The creature heard a shuffling sound. She blinked again—and then the girl was gone, because all the creature could see was a white muzzle with a black nose nearly touching her own. The earthy scent of fur nearly overwhelmed the creature, and she suddenly remembered the beast. For just a second, she felt afraid. But this beast had found her underneath that bush. This beast had rescued her.

She closed her eyes again. A moment later, she felt a tongue begin to clean her, a wonderful, familiar sensation. The creature dozed off, feeling content and safe.

For days, the creature drifted in and out of consciousness. Sometimes she woke up alone. But usually, someone was there. The person who smelled like soap, who the creature soon learned was called Dr. Li, and her assistants, Carl and Penelope. The creature would do her best to wake up for them, especially when they had bottles of delicious milk.

But she looked forward to visits from the girl and the beast even more than she looked forward to eating.

She quickly learned that their names were Mina and Niko. The creature would be dozing, and then she'd hear Carl or Penelope say, "Well, hello again, Mina and Niko!" And suddenly the creature would feel wide-awake.

Mina's face would appear first, her eyes lighting up when she saw the creature was awake. Then Niko's furry face would pop up, nose twitching as she gave the creature a thorough sniffing, followed by another tongue bath.

"Niko's so good with her," Penelope said during one of their visits. "I always think of huskies as being strong and fast—because of the racing, you know? Sometimes I forget how gentle and caring they can be."

Mina nodded. "Niko's especially good at it, since she's the leader of the pack." She paused, watching Niko lick the creature. "Wait, do you hear that?"

The room fell silent. Even Niko fell still, ears perked up. The creature heard the sound, too—but it was another few seconds before she realized it was coming from *her*.

Purrrrrrrr.

"She's purring!" Mina giggled, leaning over the creature. "Aww, she's so cute!"

Dr. Li looked pleased. "I have to say, I'm amazed at her progress. She's doing so much better now, and I really think you and Niko spending time with her over the last week has made all the difference."

The creature blinked as Niko's face appeared, blocking her view of the others. *Husky*, the creature thought, turning the word over in her mind. Niko had soft gray-and-white fur, pointy ears, and a black nose. Her eyes were light blue and shiny, and reflected a tiny, furry face that—*oh!*

Shifting a little bit, the creature realized she was looking at her own reflection in Niko's eyes! Her fur was gray and white, and her ears were pointy, just like Niko's. Her nose was pink instead of black, and her eyes were amber instead of blue. But there was no doubt about it.

The creature was a husky!

She felt a sudden surge of pride and purpose. Huskies were strong and fast, Penelope had said. They *raced*. Whatever that was, it sure sounded like fun.

"Dinnertime!" Carl entered the room carrying a bottle. "Mina, would you like to do the honors?"

"Of course!" Mina settled back into her chair, and the creature wiggled excitedly as Dr. Li lifted her up and placed her in the girl's waiting arms. Mina held the bottle up and smiled. "Eat up, Nukka!"

"Nukka?" Carl repeated. "Is that her name?"

Mina nodded. "Dad and I picked it last night. It's

a Nordic word that means *little sister*. Niko loves it, right Niko?"

The husky let out a short, single *"Arf!"*

Nukka, the creature thought happily. *My name is Nukka, and I am a husky.*

❄ ❄ ❄

The next morning, Nukka woke up before Dr. Li came in to check on her. Stretching her limbs, she crawled out of her soft little bed and peered out of her crate. Her tummy rumbled, and she wondered if Carl or Penelope was here yet.

Then Nukka thought of Niko. What was it she did to get a human's attention? She would make a loud, sharp sound. *Arf.*

Nukka sat in front of the door to her crate. She drew in a deep breath, then let out the loudest, sharpest sound she could muster.

"Mew!"

That didn't sound right, Nukka thought, her tail twitching a little. *Maybe if I'm louder?* She took another deep breath.

"Mew! Mew! MEEEOOOOOW!"

49

That was loud, all right. But it wasn't the sound Niko made at all! Still, a moment later the door opened and Penelope hurried over to the crate.

"Well, good morning, Nukka!" Penelope beamed at Nukka as she crouched down. "Was that your way of asking for breakfast?"

Nukka stood, rubbing her face against the crate in response. Laughing, Penelope got back up and walked to a part of the room Nukka couldn't see. A moment later, she reappeared—not with a bottle, but with something wider and flatter. Nukka caught a whiff of something delicious and let out another *"Mew!"*

"Let's see how you do with a bowl of canned food," Penelope said cheerfully, unlocking the crate and setting the silver bowl down. Nukka took a tentative bite. It tasted as good as it looked, and she gobbled it all up. She could just make out her reflection in the bottom of the silver bowl. Pointy ears. Gray-and-white fur. Pink nose. *Husky*, she thought, feeling reassured as she licked the bowl dry.

After Nukka finished her breakfast, Penelope

lifted her up and carried her to Dr. Li's office. "She was awake and hungry when I walked in," Penelope said, handing Nukka to the vet. "I can't believe how much she's improved!"

Dr. Li smiled, stroking Nukka's back. "Logan and Mina are on their way over to check on her. I think she might be ready to go home with them today!"

Nukka's ears perked up. Go home? Was she going to live with Mina and Niko? A deep purr rumbled from her chest, and Dr. Li and Penelope laughed.

Nukka kept Dr. Li company as she worked at her desk. But she kept glancing at the door, waiting for Mina and Niko to arrive. Finally, she heard the jingle of the bells that always meant someone had walked into the vet's office. A moment later, Nukka smelled the unmistakable scent of Niko's fur, and she attempted to crawl out of Dr. Li's lap and nearly fell to the floor.

"Whoa, there!" Dr. Li caught Nukka right in time, holding her close. "You're extra feisty today, Nukka!"

They left the office and found Mina, her dad, and Niko in the lobby talking to Penelope. The moment Nukka saw them, her tail went twitch, twitch, twitch.

Mina beamed at her. "Nukka! Penelope just told us you didn't need a bottle this morning!"

"I gave her a bowl of special canned food just for kittens, and she licked it clean," Penelope said, giving Nukka a little scratch behind her ears. "I'm going to miss this little girl!"

Mina looked confused. "Where's she going?" she asked anxiously, and Nukka suddenly felt nervous, too. But Mina's dad was smiling.

"She's ready?" he asked.

Dr. Li nodded and held Nukka out to Mina. "She's ready to go home."

Mina blinked several times. Then an enormous smile spread across her face. "Really, Dad?" she squealed, reaching for Nukka. "I didn't—I wasn't—*thank* you!"

She took Nukka gently, then knelt down so that they were both at eye level with Niko, who had been sitting patiently at Mina's side. "What do you think, Niko?" Mina asked. "Should we make Nukka part of the pack?"

For some reason, that made everyone laugh. But Niko looked appraisingly at Nukka. For a second, Nukka thought she saw a worried look flash in the husky's eyes. But then Niko's expression softened.

"*Arf!*"

"*Mew!*" Nukka responded, and that got another laugh. She really needed to work on that. But at the moment, she wasn't worried about it.

She was going *home*.

As Mina's dad scheduled a time for Nukka to visit Dr. Li again, Mina held Nukka close and talked. And talked. And *talked*. Nukka remembered the way Mina had been when Nukka was sick— quiet and solemn. But apparently that was only how she behaved when she was upset. Now that she was happy, it was like she couldn't keep the words from spilling out of her mouth.

"Mom's just going to *love* you. She had a cat when she was little—I think her name was Ginger, because she was orange. And Niko and I will introduce you to the whole pack! Suka, Kodiak—he's huge, but don't be scared, he's the sweetest—and all the pups, too! They're not much older than you. There's Klondike, Miska, Nanuk—oh, and Sakari, she's their mom. And I'll show you my room! I hope you like music. Niko and I listen to ClockWork all the time. That's my favorite band. They're—"

"Ready to go?" Mina's dad called.

Mina beamed. "We're ready!"

Nukka was still thinking about everything Mina had said as they left the office. She hadn't understood most of it—music? Band? And Mina had mentioned that her mother had a cat, whatever that was.

But one word Nukka had understood was *pack*. Pack meant family. And Niko was the leader of the pack. Nukka felt a jolt of excitement and nervousness.

What if the rest of the pack didn't like her?

"This is our truck," Mina told Nukka as she opened the door. Niko leaped inside, squeezing between the two front seats and settling down in the back seat. Mina climbed in next, carefully holding Nukka close as she strapped a belt around her waist. "Niko and all the huskies usually ride in the back. But you'll ride up front with me."

Nukka squirmed in Mina's lap as the truck came to life with a familiar *ROOOAARRR*. So *this* was one of the giant beasts she'd heard when she was lying under that bush! It was thrilling and terrifying to be inside one. But Mina and her dad seemed fine, and Niko was obviously relaxed. So Nukka tried to relax, too.

But she couldn't seem to stop wriggling.

"Nukka!" Mina giggled. "You're such a wiggle worm today!"

At last, the truck came to a stop. "Ah, Mom's got a welcome party outside!" Mina's dad exclaimed, opening his door.

Mina quickly unbuckled her seat belt, then held Nukka up so she could see. "Look, Nukka! The whole pack is waiting for you!"

Nukka stopped wriggling. Through the window,

she saw a pretty house painted yellow and white and surrounded by impossibly tall trees and lots and lots of grass. A woman who looked an awful lot like an older Mina stood in front of the house, waving and smiling. And all around her, playing in the grass, were huskies.

Some were Niko's size. Some were much bigger. But some were little—almost as little as Nukka! They did more than wriggle. They pounced, hopped, and romped. Two gray pups played tug-of-war with an old rope, while a black-and-white pup sprinted in circles, clamping a bright red ball in his mouth.

"Ready?" Mina asked Nukka. But ready or not, she was already climbing out of the truck and carrying Nukka over to the pack, with Niko trotting along at their side. Mina's mom said something, but Nukka barely heard her—all her focus was on the pack.

And as she got closer, all the pack's focus was on *her*.

Mina set Nukka down on the grass. The littlest huskies bounded over, followed by the bigger ones.

Nukka froze, hardly daring to blink as the pack surrounded her.

"Um," Mina said, sounding suddenly nervous. "Maybe this wasn't the best idea..."

"It's fine!" Mina's mom said. "The pups wouldn't hurt a fly. Go ahead, introduce her!"

Mina took a deep breath. "Okay, guys. Say hello to Nukka—your new sister!"

The bright red ball fell from the black-and-white pup's mouth. Dozens of pairs of light blue eyes stared at Nukka in disbelief.

"I think they like her," Mina said, clearly relieved.

But Nukka wasn't so sure.

Chapter Seven

Niko

Niko gazed calmly at her pack.

Suka caught her eye and tilted her head. "A kitten? Seriously?"

Klondike, a black-and-white pup who was the biggest and rowdiest of his litter, crouched down. Then he hop-hop-hopped all the way over to Nukka, who remained as still as a stone. Every muscle in the tiny kitten's body tensed as Klondike sniffed her curiously, and Niko shot the pup a warning look.

"Play nice, Klondike. She's your sister."

Klondike's fuzzy head jerked up. "Sister?! She doesn't even look like us!"

"He has a point." Suka stepped forward, staring down at the kitten. Suka's posture wasn't threatening, but Niko could tell Nukka was intimidated by the way she shrank back. A short, light yip from Niko stopped Suka in her tracks.

Niko moved to stand right next to Nukka. She surveyed the pack, making eye contact with each and every husky. "Don't judge Nukka by her looks. She's part of the pack now, and that's that."

Kodiak had been sitting at the back of the pack, observing quietly. Now he got on all fours and lumbered forward. The pups scrambled to get out of his way. Nukka trembled slightly as Kodiak leaned down until they were nose to nose. He opened his mouth, revealing a tongue nearly as big as the kitten's entire body, and then—

SLOOORP!

The kiss knocked Nukka right onto her side! She lay on her back like a turtle, four tiny paws wiggling in the air as Mina and her parents laughed. Klondike leaned forward with his rump in the air, tail wagging frantically as Nukka struggled to roll over. The moment she did, he pounced, sending both of them rolling across the frosty grass.

The other pups joined in, and Niko was pleased to see that Nukka appeared to be having fun now. She gave Suka a knowing look.

"See?"

Suka let out a dainty snort in response. "Fine. She's one of the pack."

"All right." Dad clapped his hands once. "First snow of the year was a light one, but I hear we're getting a lot more later this week. You know what that means..."

Niko stared at him eagerly, waiting for him to say her favorite words.

"Training runs!" Dad exclaimed.

"Woof!" Kodiak's deep, booming bark startled the pups. Nukka, who'd been tussling with Klondike, stood stock-still, fur rising along her back.

Niko gave a short bark in response, her tail wagging. She glanced at Nukka to make sure she understood, but the kitten still looked confused and slightly frightened by the sudden change in energy. Suka noticed it, too.

"She doesn't speak our language, Niko."

Niko dipped her head. "Not yet. But she'll learn."

❄ ❄ ❄

The weekend passed quickly. Niko spent most of Sunday morning sitting on the back porch, watching the pups play with Nukka. Every once in a while, she'd let out a commanding yip if she thought the huskies were getting a little too rambunctious. Nukka seemed to be perfectly healthy now, but Niko couldn't forget what the kitten had looked like under that bush, fragile and sick.

Besides, even a healthy kitten was no match for a growing husky pup. Klondike and his brothers and sisters would start training to be sled dogs soon. They'd get strong and fast, while Nukka stayed at home and . . .

Niko considered this. What *did* cats do? She had no idea. The Fergusons next door had a cat named Lola, but Niko didn't know her very well. She only came outside when the weather was warm, usually to sunbathe on the Fergusons' front porch.

Niko watched as Nukka tumbled a few feet,

rolled over, shook herself off, then chased Miska across the grass. She couldn't imagine Nukka lazing around on the porch all day, but surely she'd want to, right? Once again, Niko felt a twinge of anxiety. She had no problem leading her pack, keeping the huskies in line, training the pups. And she meant what she told the others—Niko considered Nukka one of the pack.

But as Suka had pointed out, Nukka was a different species. And Niko wasn't entirely sure she knew how to raise her. Still, Niko was the pack leader, and it was up to her to figure it out.

The patio door slid open, and Mina stepped outside. "Brought you a sandwich, Dad," she said, and Niko caught a whiff of turkey as she held out something wrapped in a napkin.

"Thanks, sweetie!" Dad was sitting at the long wooden table Mr. Ferguson had built for him a few years ago, working on his laptop. Niko gave a hopeful wag when Mina turned to smile at her.

"I didn't forget you, Niko!" Mina held out a small brown cube, and Niko's mouth filled with saliva when the scent of peanut butter hit her nose. She gobbled it down eagerly, and Mina gave her a quick scratch behind the ears.

"What are you working on, Dad?"

"Mapping out a route for our first training run," Dad said, and Niko's tail automatically went thump-thump-thump on the patio. *Training run!*

"Are you taking the pups on the first run?" Mina asked.

"Absolutely," Dad replied. "It'll be an easy one. Actually, I think I'm going to start dragline training this week."

Mina giggled, and Niko knew why. A litter's first dragline was almost always funny. Huskies had to run fast while pulling a lot of weight. When a litter was over two months old, Dad would strap harnesses onto the pups for a few minutes every day so they would get used to the feeling. Once they were four months old, he would attach an extra-long leash to their harnesses, then tie the leash around a plank of wood. The puppy would then try to run, dragging the plank of wood behind them.

At least, that's what was supposed to happen. But the first time always resulted in silly behavior. Sometimes the puppy would just sit there, as if the plank was as unmovable as a house. Other times, the puppy would take off in a joyful run, only to reel back when the leash went tight and the plank proved too heavy for them to move. Niko remembered Kodiak's first dragline vividly. The burly pup had started off at a slow trot, dragging the plank behind him, and Mina and her parents had cheered. Then Kodiak had glanced behind him, seen the plank, and thought it was chasing him! He'd sprinted in a giant circle around the yard for nearly five minutes, yipping frantically as the plank chugged along dutifully behind him. Mina had laughed so hard she'd slumped over onto Niko, hiccupping into her fur.

Of course, Kodiak had gotten the hang of it eventually. As funny as his performance had been, Niko had known instantly that he'd be a perfect wheel dog. The wheel dogs were at the back of the line closest to the sled. When the team started running, the wheel dogs would pull the weight of the sled first, so they had to be extra strong. Kodiak had pulled that plank of wood easily at just four months old. Niko gazed out at the playing pups, wondering which positions they'd end up taking. Klondike seemed to have lead dog potential, she thought, watching as he led the rest of the litter in a race around the yard.

"Dad!" Mina exclaimed suddenly, pointing. "Look at Nukka!"

Niko looked, too, and for a moment she thought her eyes must be playing tricks on her. Nukka was trotting straight toward Klondike, a stick clamped between her teeth. Niko blinked, then blinked again. She'd definitely never seen Lola carrying a stick before. This was not catlike behavior.

Nukka paused mid-trot, and so did Klondike Then the puppy pounced at the kitten, and she turned and sprinted gleefully across the grass. Klondike overtook her quickly, his jaws clamping down on one end of the stick. He tugged, but Nukka tugged back, planting her paws firmly and giving her head a little shake.

Dad laughed. "A kitten and a puppy playing tug-of-war. Well, now I've seen everything."

Mina pulled out her phone and started to record the antics. She was giggling so hard she could barely speak. "I can't wait to show this to Emily!"

Niko glanced up at Mina. She'd stopped laughing now, and her shoulders slumped as she lowered her phone. The change in her energy was as abrupt as when the pack heard Dad say the word *Dinnertime!*

Dad noticed, too. He kept his tone light, but he watched Mina carefully. "I haven't seen Emily since school started. Why don't you ask her over for dinner tonight? I'm sure she'd love to meet Nukka!"

Niko sat up hopefully, wagging her tail. But Mina just shrugged.

"I think Emily's busy today."

"Ah." Dad was silent for a moment. "You know, we were so busy taking care of Nukka all last week that I didn't get to hear much about your first week of school. How'd it go?"

"Fine," Mina said, keeping her eyes on the pups and Nukka.

Dad hesitated. "Are you sure? Because—"

"Everything's *fine*, Dad!" Mina sounded exasperated. "Anyway, I'm busy, too. I want to finish that new shirt design before dinner."

With that, she marched back into the house. Niko saw her own worry reflected in Dad's expression.

Whatever was going on with Mina and Emily, it definitely wasn't *fine*.

Chapter Eight

Mina

Mina lay sprawled on her bed, watching for probably the tenth time the video she'd taken of Nukka romping around with the stick in her mouth. She thought about sending it to Emily; she would think it was just as funny as Mina did. Maybe she'd respond with a laughing emoji, and then Mina would text, Want to come over and meet Nukka? Mom's making chowder for dinner!

What would Emily's response be?

Sorry, I can't tonight! ☹

Or maybe...

Sorry! I can, but I'd rather hang out with anyone but you.

Sighing, Mina dropped her phone on her bed-spread. Emily would never say anything so mean. But she'd made it pretty clear all last week that she didn't want to spend time with Mina anymore. She sat with the F Twins at lunch every day. She picked Fiona as her science lab partner, and she teamed up with Faith for relay racing during gym. And Friday morning, the three of them had showed up to school wearing matching cord necklaces, each with a different charm: a wolf for Faith, an owl for Fiona, and a unicorn for Emily. Mina was half expecting her to change her name to Femily so they could call themselves the F Triplets.

Mina didn't mind Emily having other friends. After all, Mina had other friends, too—no one she was nearly as close to as Emily, but perfectly nice friends. Like Jacob in her English class who wrote really good poetry, or Lila and Bianca, who let Mina sit with them at lunch and even invited her to join their book club. So, really, Mina was perfectly fine with Emily hanging out with the F Twins.

But why didn't Emily want to hang out with

Mina? Emily wasn't acting mad—in fact, she almost looked like she felt guilty sometimes. What had Mina done to push her best friend away?

The door to Mina's bedroom creaked open. She glanced up as Niko slipped inside. The husky leaped nimbly onto the bed and curled into a ball at Mina's side. Mina scratched Niko behind the left ear, a spot guaranteed to get her back leg wiggling. Sure enough, Niko squeezed her eyes closed as her leg started to thump-thump-thump against the comforter.

Normally, this routine made Mina smile. But right now, her throat felt too tight. She knew Dad could tell something weird was going on with Emily. Niko must have picked up on it, too, if she'd left the puppies outside playing to check up on her. Mina was grateful that Dad hadn't pressed her for more information.

She didn't want to talk about the fact that she'd started seventh grade without a best friend.

❄ ❄ ❄

When Mina's alarm went off the next morning, she wondered whether her parents would let her stay home if she pretended to be sick. They'd probably see right through her, Mina decided with a defeated sigh. She'd never been a good liar.

In the kitchen, Dad was already stirring a giant vat of homemade dog food. Mina remembered the first time Emily had been over when Dad had been making it. She'd snuck a spoonful when no one was looking, then didn't believe them when they told her she'd just eaten dog food.

"Don't worry!" Mina had said between giggles, when Emily looked like she might actually cry. "It's just ground meat, yams, and carrots, stuff like that. It's people food, too!"

It had been an inside joke between them through elementary school. On chili dog day, Emily would take a giant bite, swallow, then announce, "I've literally had dog food that tasted better than this," and the two of them would collapse into giggles.

"Morning, sweetie!" Dad finished ladling spoon-fuls of dog food into small bowls for the puppies. "Help me with these?"

"Sure!" Mina loved watching the pack eat.

Kodiak would be licking his bowl clean ten seconds after she'd put it down in front of him. "I'll get a bowl for Nukka's food."

After loading the food onto two giant trays, Mina followed Dad to the porch and began setting the bowls down. She could see the huskies roaming around the yard, a few still taking care of their morning business. Klondike was already tearing around in circles, sending blades of grass flying behind him. After a few seconds, Mina spotted Nukka, too. The kitten was standing stock-still, her bright amber eyes tracking Klondike's path. Mina couldn't help thinking it looked as if Nukka was studying the puppy.

"Breakfast time!" Dad called, stepping back from the bowls. The reaction was immediate: Every fuzzy head whipped around to stare at him, and then the stampede began. Mina grinned when she saw that the puppies were doing their best to keep up with the bigger dogs as they raced toward the porch. Then her eyes widened.

"Dad, look at Nukka!"

The kitten was charging alongside the pups. She reached the bowls a split second after the last pup, gave her bowl of canned food a sniff...then moved to Klondike's bowl.

"Hey, now!" Dad looked as surprised as Mina felt. Nukka was gobbling up the dog food—she *liked* it! In fact...

"Dad, she's wagging her tail!"

Mina couldn't believe what she was seeing. The tiny kitten's tail was high in the air, swaying back and forth just like the puppies' tails.

"Eating dog food won't make her sick, will it?" Mina asked.

Dad shook his head. "No, but I'll look up homemade cat food recipes to make for tomorrow, just to be sure she's getting the nutrition a kitten needs."

"What's going on?" Mom joined them on the porch, cupping a mug of steaming coffee in her hands. Mina pointed at Nukka, who seemed to be in a race with Klondike to see who could eat the fastest.

"Guess we didn't need to worry about whether our new kitten would fit in with the pack," Dad said.

Mom took a sip of coffee and smiled. "I'm not sure our new kitten even realizes she's a kitten."

Mina thought Mom might be right. Nukka was quickly becoming part of the family, and before long, Mina couldn't imagine not having the kitten around.

But Nukka was definitely exhibiting some interesting behavior. Like on Tuesday, when Mina trudged home from school and opened the front door, Niko bounded in from the next room, jumping up and placing her paws on Mina's chest for a hug, like she did every day. Mina wrapped her arms around the husky's fuzzy neck ... and felt a pair of teeny-tiny claws digging into her jeans. She looked down in surprise to find Nukka standing on her hind legs, gazing up at her beseechingly. Giggling, Mina scooped the kitten up and gave her a gentle hug, too.

Then there was playtime for the husky pups.

Mina would watch in amazement as Nukka jumped into the fray without hesitation, wrestling her brothers and sisters, playing tug-of-war with chew toys, pouncing on balls with her tail wagging frantically. Klondike and the other pups were bigger and stronger, but Nukka's tiny size gave her an advantage in some of their games. When the pups would pile up on their favorite rope toy, Nukka could squeeze in and make off with the toy before the rest of the litter knew what had happened. After a good wrestling match, Nukka would sit on her haunches just like Klondike, tongue hanging out as she panted happily.

"She's not strong, but she's slippery," Mom observed one night over a dinner of grilled halibut and baked potatoes, watching Nukka, Miska, and Klondike bat a tennis ball around the kitchen. "And totally fearless."

But it was the bath incident that gave Mina an idea.

It started on Friday after school, when Mina shook out her sopping-wet umbrella on the porch before stepping inside the house. Niko greeted her with the usual hug, but Nukka was nowhere to be seen.

"Mom? Dad?" Mina called, heading into the kitchen. "Uh-oh…" Tiny, muddy paw prints covered the tile floors, and the back door was slightly open. "Niko, any idea what's going on?"

Niko padded over to the door and stuck her nose outside, while Mina peeked through the window. The rain had slowed to a frosty sprinkle, and the patch of dirt near the patio had turned into a mud puddle. And wriggling around in that puddle, having the time of their lives, were the husky puppies.

"Dad!" Mina called, and she heard footsteps coming down the hall. But she was already running outside, umbrella forgotten. "Oh boy, you guys are going to be in so much trouble!" she chided the pups. "Look how filthy you—*Nukka!*"

Mina froze openmouthed, gazing down at the puddle. The tiny kitten was so muddy, all Mina could really see were her bright amber eyes. Dad caught up to her with a curious Kodiak at his side, and burst out laughing.

"Didn't realize I was raising a litter of piglets!"

Still chuckling, he headed inside to get his and Mina's raincoats. Then the two of them spent almost fifteen minutes attempting to round up the squirming, slippery pups and kitten. Suka joined Niko on the porch, and Mina could have sworn the two huskies looked amused at the litter's antics.

"Mom's running a bath," Dad told Mina over his shoulder as they headed inside. "It's going to take a while to get these guys all clean. I've never seen such a mess!"

"Wait—a bath?" Mina stopped just inside the bathroom. "What about Nukka?"

"What do you mean?" Mom asked, helping Dad lower his armload of happy pups into the warm water. Mina moved closer, holding out Miska with one hand. In her other hand, Nukka eyed the bathtub.

"Cats hate water," Mina said. "Remember when Lola next door had fleas? Mrs. Ferguson showed me the scratches on her arms after she tried giving her a bath. She said Lola was like a tornado with claws!"

"Hmm, good point." Mom scooted over so that Mina had room to kneel down next to the tub. "Well, bring her over here and let's see what she thinks."

Dad leaned back on the counter, watching as Mina carefully placed Nukka on the edge of the tub. The mud-covered kitten stood very still, watching the pups splash around in the shallow water.

"I don't know," Mina said after a moment. "Maybe we need to—oh!"

Without warning, Nukka leaped right into the tub with a tiny splash! She surfaced quickly, blinking as water streamed down her furry face. Then she wagged her tail, sending droplets of water flying, and splish-splashed her way over to where Klondike was nosing a bar of soap around the bottom of the tub.

Mom shook her head. "Unbelievable. A kitten who loves baths!"

"She really does think she's a husky," Mina said with a giggle. "She copies everything Niko does! And she's always trying to keep up with Klondike."

"You know, this reminds me of that funny story we saw on the news last year," Dad said. "Remember that porpoise who saved a dog's life in Maine?"

"Oh, yeah!" Mina exclaimed. "They became friends. And then that girl and her dog helped the porpoise find his pod!"

"But I don't remember anything about the porpoise thinking it was a dog. Although I guess the girl would've had a hard time walking him on a leash," Dad added, laughing.

Leaning over, Mom splashed a little water over Nukka. The kitten batted at her hand, enjoying herself. "I think she just wants to fit in with her new pack," Mom said. "And she's doing a great job!"

Mina blinked, staring at the soaking-wet kitten. Before she'd ended up under that bush, she'd had a pack of her own—a litter of kittens, and a mama cat, too. But now, she was part of the husky pack, and she was adapting.

Maybe Mina could do the same thing. If she could fit in with Emily and the F Twins, they might welcome her into the pack. Mina just had to adapt.

Chapter Nine

NUKKA

Nukka leaped ahead of the pack, feeling the collar strain around her neck. She slowed automatically and allowed the leash Mina was holding to go slack. A second later, Klondike rushed past her and clambered over a gnarled root.

"Can't catch me!"

As Klondike's head poked up over the root, Nukka crouched, sticking her rear in the air and wagging her tail. Then she bounded forward and leaped nimbly over the root.

"Nukka!" Mina cried as the leash slipped from her hand. Nukka could hear Mina's laughter as she crashed into Klondike, sending him rolling across the frost and pine needles scattered over the forest floor. Nukka landed daintily on her feet and waited for Mina to catch up, feeling pleased with herself.

"You're right, she loves the leash," Mom said with a chuckle. She was holding Miska's and Nanuk's leashes, with Niko ambling along leash-free at her side. Mina was holding Nukka's and Klondike's leashes—or at least, she had been until Klondike had started a game of tag.

Purrrr. Nukka heard it at the same moment as Klondike did. He tilted his head sideways and gave her a questioning look.

"What's that noise you're always making?"

Nukka's tail twitched, and she tried to force the sound to stop. "None of your business."

She couldn't seem to control the purr noise. It simply happened when she was happy. And she was happy a lot. But none of the other husky pups made that noise, no matter how happy they were. They wagged their tails and pounced around and Miska would sometimes let out a high-pitched whine if Dad pulled out the jar of peanut butter treats. Nukka had tried to imitate Miska's whine once, but it had come out more like *yowwwwwl!* and Niko and Mina had come running, both looking slightly panicked.

Niko didn't look panicked now. But she did look concerned. "Did you hurt yourself? That was quite a jump!"

"I'm fine!" Nukka licked her paw, removing a tiny pine needle. It hadn't felt like a particularly big jump. Sometimes she worried Niko still saw her as the sick, half-starved creature she'd found under the bush. But Nukka was totally healthy now! And she *loved* jumping. She was glad Niko hadn't been in Mina's room this morning, when Nukka had attempted to jump from Mina's bed onto her dresser. She hadn't quite made it, and had scrabbled at the edge for a few frantic seconds before falling to the carpet with a soft plop. It hadn't hurt, but Nukka had a feeling Niko would have made a much bigger deal out of it.

When they reached a small field, Mom and Mina let the pups off their leashes for a little play-time. Klondike raced across the grass, with Miska and Nanuk right behind him. But before Nukka could follow, Niko nipped lightly at her back legs.

"Stay here for a minute."

Nukka felt slightly annoyed, but she didn't argue. Instead, she sat next to Niko while Mina and Mom strolled around the edge of the field, keeping an eye on the pups.

"That noise you make sometimes is called a purr."

Surprised, Nukka turned to look at Niko. "Oh. Why don't the other pups do it?"

"Because . . ." Niko paused. "Because dogs don't purr, Nukka. Cats do. And you are a cat. A kitten, to be more precise."

Cat. Kitten. This wasn't the first time Nukka had heard those words. She knew, deep down, that she wasn't exactly like the other huskies. "But I'm still part of the pack, right?"

Niko settled more comfortably on the grass. "Of course you are!"

"So I can go on training runs and learn to race just like Klondike, right?"

Nukka waited anxiously for Niko to reassure her. But the husky was quiet for a long moment.

"Sled racing is difficult and dangerous, Nukka. Kittens aren't built for that kind of—"

"But you said I was part of the pack!" Nukka felt frustrated. "If you really meant it, you'd let me race!"

Niko looked at her sharply. "You are one of the pack, Nukka. But you are not a husky, and I will not put you in danger."

Nukka wanted to argue, but she knew it would do no good. She watched, feeling resentful and rebellious, as Mom and Mina herded the pups back over. Maybe she looked like a cat on the outside, but she felt like a husky on the inside. Didn't that count for anything?

"We'd better head back," Mom said as Mina scooped up the leashes. "Dad wanted to start dragline training at three, and I've got to get dinner ready."

"Okay!" Mina knelt and scratched Klondike behind the ears. "I bet you're going to love dragline training, Klondike!" Nukka hurried over, butting her head against Mina's leg, and Mina laughed. "So will you, Nukka," she added. But her tone had changed a little, like she was making a joke. Nukka could feel Niko's gaze, but she ignored her.

When they reached the house, Nukka saw that Dad was already in the yard with the other huskies. Kodiak was busily gnawing on a rawhide bone twice as big as Nukka, while Suka and Sakari sat on the porch, their light blue eyes fixed on Dad. He was attaching what looked like super-long leashes to planks of wood.

Nukka came to a halt. "What is this?"

Instead of responding, Niko trotted past Nukka, then sat neatly at Dad's side. Nukka, Klondike, and the other pups scurried after her and settled down on the grass to watch.

First, Dad strapped Niko into her harness. Next, he attached the super-long leash to the harness, leaving the leash in a loose coil on the grass. Then he moved back, giving Niko lots of room.

The air suddenly felt thick with anticipation.

Nukka felt the fur rise along her back as all eyes turned to Niko. The husky stood perfectly still, but Nukka could see that all her muscles were tense.

"Hike!" Dad shouted.

Niko took off, sprinting across the yard, the super-long leash uncoiling behind her. When stretched taut, the plank of wood took off through the grass after the husky. Nukka watched, fascinated, as Niko dragged the plank in a perfect circle around the yard, finally looping back to her starting place. Dad tossed a treat in the air, and Niko caught it easily, sitting down in a more relaxed position.

This is training to pull the sled, Nukka realized, her heart thumping faster.

"Klondike!" Dad called, beckoning to the puppy. "You're up, little guy!"

"I'm first, I'm first, I'm first!" Klondike swaggered over to Dad, attempting to lick his hands as Dad strapped on his harness and attached the leash. Nukka watched closely as Dad stepped back and held up a tennis ball. Klondike went still, eyes fixed on his favorite toy.

"Hike!" Dad shouted, throwing the ball across the yard.

Klondike flew after the ball, bounding joyfully through the grass. "Mine-mine-mine-mine-mine!" Klondike panted. Nukka's gaze moved to the plank as the leash went tight. "Mine-mine—*ACK!*"

Klondike let out a very un-Klondike-like squeak, surprising even himself, and he spun around to stare at the plank. It lay still on the grass, and Klondike eyed it suspiciously before taking off after the ball again.

"Arf!" The moment he felt the resistance, Klondike spun around again.

Pull! Nukka thought. *That's what they want you to do. Drag it around like Niko did, like a sled.*

Klondike seemed to be thinking carefully, too. Then he ambled over and began to gnaw at the leash, trying to free the plank. Mina burst out laughing as Dad hurried over to stop him.

"Nice try, little guy," Dad said with a grin, unhooking the leash from Klondike's harness. "Miska, let's see what you think!"

Suddenly, a slinky movement caught Nukka's eye. Turning, she squinted at the Fergusons' house. There was no fence between the two backyards—the Fergusons didn't have any dogs, and they never seemed to mind when the huskies strayed over into their yard.

At least, Nukka had thought they didn't have a dog. But something was moving slowly through the grass. Something with black-and-brown fur and yellow eyes that seemed to glow. They locked onto Nukka's eyes, and her fur rose.

"Hike!"

Startled, Nukka whipped around just in time to see Miska tentatively trotting away from the plank, leash uncoiling behind her. When the leash went taut, the plank jerked forward a few inches. Then Miska stopped and sat primly, looking at Dad for further instructions.

Keep going! Nukka thought, but Miska refused to budge again until Dad unhooked the leash. Coming to a decision, Nukka padded over the grass toward them.

"All right," Dad said, straightening up. "Nanuk, how about—oh!"

He looked down at Nukka as she rubbed her head against his ankle. Mina was giggling again. "I think she wants a turn!"

Kneeling, Dad tickled Nukka behind the ear. "Aw. That plank weighs more than you, Nukka! I don't want you to hurt yourself."

Nukka sat next to the plank, avoiding Niko's gaze. She *was* a husky, no matter what Niko said. And she was determined to prove it.

"What about this?" Mina picked up one of Kodiak's worn-down rawhide bones. "It's way lighter than the plank. Nukka could probably drag this."

Dad smiled. "Why not?"

Nukka watched eagerly as Dad tied the leash around the bone. As he was strapping her into the harness, Nukka remembered the creature in the Fergusons' yard. She looked over and saw those glowing eyes still gazing at her without blinking.

Dad set Nukka on all fours, and she told herself to focus. Niko and the rest of the pack were all watching. Nukka stood very still, tensed to run at Dad's command.

"Hike!"

Nukka took off at a run, but not too fast—she remembered what had happened to Klondike, and she braced herself for the weight of the bone.

Oof! It felt like an invisible force yanking hard on her harness. Determined, Nukka kept going, one paw in front of the other. Her run had slowed to a trot, but she was still going.

"Dad, she's doing it!" Mina cried, and the amazement in her voice filled Nukka with confidence. She dragged the bone in a wide circle around the yard, just like Niko had done. When she reached Dad and Mina, they both clapped and cheered. Nukka was pleased to see that Niko looked impressed. Even Suka dipped her head slightly when Nukka looked her way.

"Nice job!"

Panting heavily, Nukka wagged her tail as Dad unclasped her harness. It wasn't until Dad had strapped Nanuk in that Nukka looked back over at the Fergusons' yard. But the creature with the yellow eyes was gone.

Dad gave the other pups another try at the dragline. All three did much better, but Nukka knew she'd been the best. And when Dad began strapping the huskies into harnesses for a quick run before dinner, Nukka literally leaped at the chance.

"Whoa!" Mina cried as Nukka snatched a harness between her teeth and scurried around in a circle. "Sorry, Nukka. No pups or kitties on this run."

Sure enough, Nukka saw that Mom was bringing the other pups into the house. She dropped the harness and looked from the house to the sled. Then Nukka sprinted toward the sled and jumped inside.

Mina burst out laughing, and Dad chuckled, too. "Well, it's only for a few miles," he said to Mina. "Think you can hold on to her for the ride?"

"Yeah!" Mina scrambled into the sled and scooped Nukka up, holding her in her lap. Nukka felt the happy rumble in her chest—a *purr*, Niko had called it—and suddenly, she was filled with doubt.

Dogs don't purr. Cats do. And you are a cat.

Nukka watched as the pack arranged themselves in two straight lines with Niko at the front. Once Dad had checked each of their harnesses, he climbed onto the sled behind Mina. A moment later:

"Mush!"

The pack surged forward with the sled at an alarmingly fast speed. Nukka let out a mew of surprise that she couldn't even hear over the rush of the wind. They sped into the woods, the sled bumping over the snow-covered path.

"What do you think, Nukka?" Mina called, holding the kitten up so she could see better. Nukka squinted against the freezing wind and watched the huskies, legs pumping, tongues lolling, occasionally letting out a happy bark. The path curved ahead, and Nukka watched as Suka veered to Niko's left when they took the turn. The huskies shifted over in response to Suka, and once the sled had rounded the turn, they shifted back into straight lines. Through a clearing in the trees ahead, Nukka caught a glimpse of a snow-covered mountain range. She imagined the pack racing into those mountains, covering miles and miles and working together as a team, and she felt a pang of longing. Riding in the sled was fun. But one day, Klondike and the other pups would be racing along this path. And Nukka wanted to race with them.

You are a cat, she heard Niko say in her mind.

No, I'm not, Nukka thought fiercely. *I am a husky.*

Chapter Ten

Mina

On Monday, school seemed to drag on even more than usual. Mina sat with Lila and Bianca at lunch, half listening as they talked about a fantasy book they were both reading, and trying not to look over at the table where Emily sat with the F Twins. When Mina went to throw away her trash, she couldn't help overhearing some of their conversation.

"You guys want to meet in the food court at six?" Fiona was saying, toying with the owl charm on her necklace. "That way we can get some pizza before the movie."

"Sounds good!" Emily agreed. She kept talking, but laughter from another table covered up whatever she said, and by the time it died down, Mina had reached the trash cans.

But she'd heard more than enough to put her plan into action.

That evening, Mina sat nervously in Dad's truck, stroking Nukka's back. The kitten had curled up into a ball for her usual post-dinner nap. When Dad pulled up outside the mall's main entrance, he gave Mina a big smile.

"Have fun, sweetie," he said. "And tell Emily the pack misses her!"

Mina swallowed hard. "I will!"

She climbed out of the truck carefully, still holding Nukka. She hadn't lied to Dad, exactly— she was meeting Emily in the food court, after all. But she'd made it sound like Emily had invited her, which definitely wasn't the case.

Nukka perked up as Mina walked into the mall and passed the movie theater. She sniffed the air when they passed the pretzel wagon, and Mina laughed.

"You just had dinner!" she said teasingly. "I

swear, sometimes I think you'd eat more than Kodiak if we let you."

Nukka mewed in response, and Mina relaxed. Having Nukka here made her feel less nervous. And she was the perfect icebreaker, too. Surely even the F Twins couldn't resist an adorable kitten!

Mina headed into Pawlicious Pets and made a beeline for the row of dog toys. "What do you think, Nukka?" she asked, pausing in front of a display of bones, balls, and stuffed toys just for puppies. "Which one do you like?"

Nukka gazed at the selection with a serious expression. Then, with a little *"Mew!"* she batted a paw at a bright purple bone. Mina grinned.

"Perfect."

After paying for the bone, Mina threw the wrapper away. Nukka's tiny mouth clamped around the bone as soon as Mina offered it to her, and she held it tight, looking just as pleased with herself as Kodiak after getting a new rawhide.

As Mina made her way to the food court, her heart began to thump loudly. Several people pointed, laughing at the sight of the tiny kitten with the bone in her mouth, but Mina was too nervous to pay them any attention. Taking a deep breath, she entered the food court.

It took her a moment to spot Emily and the F Twins at a table near Crusty's Pizza, which had a long line. A few other kids were with them—Mina recognized them from school, but she wasn't sure of their names. The sight of them caused her stomach to twist even tighter. Why were they invited, but not Mina?

Taking great care not to look over at Emily, Mina strolled casually toward the line for Crusty's Pizza. She stroked Nukka's head with her free hand, which was shaking. *Please notice me, please notice me, please...*

"Omigod, look at that little kitty!"

Yes! Mina glanced over at the table toward the girl who'd cried out. She had curly blond hair and bright red glasses, and Mina was pretty positive she was a seventh grader. Lily, or maybe Lucy?

"Hi!" Mina only hesitated a moment before walking over. "Did you want to meet Nukka?"

"Yes, please!" Lily-or-Lucy squealed. As she jumped up, Mina glanced at the others, then pretended to be surprised when she saw Emily.

"Oh, hey!"

"Hey!" Emily was smiling, and Mina relaxed slightly. "So this is the rescue kitten, huh?"

"She's got a bone!" Fiona exclaimed, giggling. Within seconds, all the girls were clustered around Mina and Nukka, cooing and taking turns scratching the kitten under the chin. Nukka's purr made them all giggle, and when Mina told them all about how Nukka was training with her dad's huskies, they listened with rapt attention.

"Come sit with us!" Lily-or-Lucy said, beckoning for Mina to follow her to the table. "I'm Lucy, by the way. Does Nukka have an Instagram account?"

Mina blinked. "Um. No?"

"Oh my god, you should totally make one for her!" Fiona exclaimed, sitting down across the table. "Kittens and puppies get *tons* of followers. And a kitten that acts like a dog?"

"Nukka would totally be famous!" Faith agreed.

Mina had never seen the F Twins so enthusiastic. She had to admit, they were probably right.

"Hey, that's a really cool shirt," Lucy said.

Mina glanced down and beamed. "Thanks! I made it, actually." She was wearing her Zion shirt, because he was Emily's favorite member.

"Wow, really?"

"Yeah. I started a business over the summer— Mina's Original Designs. I make ClockWork shirts."

"ClockWork?" Lucy said distractedly. She was pretending to wrestle over the bone with Nukka while the other girls giggled.

"The band, yeah," Mina said. "There's six members, so I have six designs, one for each of them." She chanced a glance over at Emily, but she appeared absorbed in a conversation with Fiona. "Hey, I was going to get a slice of pizza—will you watch Nukka?"

"Yes!" Lucy held out her hands eagerly, and Mina handed Nukka over. The line was still long at Crusty's, so she passed it and headed for the restroom.

Mina couldn't believe how well this was going!

Sure, Emily hadn't really talked to her yet. But Lucy had been really nice, and all the girls were totally in love with Nukka. Maybe after tonight, Emily and the F Twins would start inviting Mina to hang out sometimes.

She was about to leave her stall when the restroom door opened, and she heard Faith's voice.

"That kitten is *so* adorable. But oh my god, when she started talking about ClockWork..." She started giggling, apparently unable to finish her sentence.

"Why is that so funny?" another girl asked. "I like that band!"

"No, you don't understand," Faith told her. "Emily and Mina used to be, like, best friends. But then Mina got totally *obsessed* with ClockWork. Emily said she literally never talked about anything else. That's why she doesn't hang out with her as much anymore. She said Mina's super nice and everything, but she couldn't stand hearing about that band for another second!"

The two kept talking and giggling, but Mina couldn't hear over the rush of blood in her ears. Her face burned with humiliation, and she felt her eyes filling up with hot tears. After a minute, the restroom door banged closed, and Mina was alone again.

She stepped out of the stall and headed to the sinks. Her hands shook as she washed them. ClockWork had been her and Emily's *thing*—it had never even occurred to Mina that the band they both loved was the reason Emily had stopped being her best friend.

Did she really talk about them that much? Mina dried her hands, and her stomach knotted up all over again as she thought about it. She had to admit, occasionally Mom's and Dad's faces would tighten when she brought up ClockWork at dinner. And then there was the way Ms. Wakefield's smile had gone kind of funny when Mina had been explaining all her shirt designs in detail at the farmers' market.

Emily said she literally never talked about anything else. Mina groaned, covering her face with her hands. Okay, fine—maybe she *did* talk about ClockWork too much. But she couldn't help herself! She'd thought Emily loved them as much as she did, but apparently, she'd been wrong.

For a second, Mina considered sneaking out of the food court and calling Dad to come pick her up early. But then she remembered Nukka, and she sighed. Her kitten fit in with Emily's friends better than she did!

Mina pictured the way Nukka had dragged that old rawhide bone around the backyard on Saturday. She wasn't nearly as strong as the husky pups, but she was really clever—in fact, she was the only one who'd copied what Niko had done on the first try.

"You can do this," she told her reflection in the mirror firmly. "You can adapt." Squaring her shoulders, Mina left the restroom and marched back to Emily and her friends. She wouldn't talk about ClockWork, no matter what. She would do whatever she had to do to fit in.

Maybe then, finally, Emily would welcome her into the pack.

Chapter Eleven

Niko

Niko was curled up on Mina's bed taking her post-dinner snooze when Suka came bounding into the room.

"Wake up!" Suka nosed Niko's face a few times, then let out a soft yip.

Mildly irritated, Niko blinked and sat up. "Is something wrong?"

"No, something's finally right!" Suka spun in a little circle, and Niko stared at her. "Mina just got home with Nukka."

Niko yawned widely, showing off all her teeth. "And?"

"She was—"

Suka fell still when Mina entered her room,

carrying a dozing Nukka. Niko noticed she was smiling as she laid Nukka down on the tiny bed next to her closet.

"Hi, Niko!" Mina came over to give Niko a hug, and that was when Niko smelled what Suka was so excited about.

Emily!

Niko felt a surge of joy. Mina had been with Emily! She watched happily as Mina took her pajamas out of the top dresser drawer and headed to the bathroom, singing "Borrowed Time" under her breath.

Suka's tail went thwap-thwap-thwap against the carpet. "She's back with her pack!"

"Thank goodness." Niko cast a glance at the tiny fuzzy ball that was Nukka. "Maybe now things will finally get back to normal."

❄ ❄ ❄

The next morning, Mina still looked as cheerful as ever. Niko groomed her paws delicately as Mina got dressed for school. Mina had just finished tying her shoelaces when she froze.

"Oh."

Niko looked up curiously. Mina headed back to her closet and pulled out a green flannel shirt. To Niko's surprise, she pulled off the ClockWork shirt she'd made and put the flannel shirt on instead. Niko couldn't help but notice that Mina seemed sad as she carefully folded the shirt and put it back in her dresser.

"Bye, Niko! Bye, Nukka!" Mina kissed them both before leaving, and Niko turned to Nukka. The kitten was sitting up on her bed, but she still looked a little drowsy.

"Did Mina have fun with Emily yesterday?"

Nukka blinked, tilting her head. "Yes, I think so! Why?"

"No reason." Niko leaped nimbly off the bed. "We'd better hurry or Kodiak will make sure there isn't any breakfast left."

But when Niko stepped out onto the patio, she forgot all about food. A fresh layer of bright white snow covered the grass completely. And right in the middle of the yard was Dad, kneeling on the snow next to his sled.

Niko let out a joyful and completely undignified *"Arf!"* and sprinted toward Dad, who laughed.

"That's right, girl! It's time for another practice run!"

Niko barked again, her tail wagging ferociously. She couldn't wait to get out in the woods again, flying down snow-covered paths.

"It's going to be a short one," Dad warned her, making a few adjustments to the rigging. "We'll be taking a few of the pups along to see how they do."

A short run was much better than no run at all. Pleased, Niko hurried back to the porch, where the puppies and Nukka were scarfing down their breakfasts. Niko joined them, nipping Klondike when he tried to run off with a little bit of food still left in his bowl. "Eat every bite! You'll need the energy for the run."

Klondike obediently licked his bowl clean, as did the rest of the pack. Nukka made a show of licking her chops once her tiny bowl was empty. "I'm ready!"

"You?" Klondike flicked his tail. "No way you're

coming on a sled run. You can't even pull a plank of wood, much less a sled!"

Nukka narrowed her eyes at him. "You can't pull a sled, either. It's a team effort. And I'm part of the team."

She very pointedly didn't look at Niko, who bristled. Did Nukka not remember their conversation? Racing was far too dangerous for a kitten. Niko thought she'd made that perfectly clear. But now Nukka was attempting to defy her, and Niko couldn't let her do that—especially not in front of the pack.

"Kodiak, Suka, bring the pups over to the sled." Niko nodded in Dad's direction. "Make sure they don't cause any trouble getting strapped up."

Once the huskies had surrounded Dad and the sled, Niko turned to Nukka. The kitten stared at her with an expression of defiance that Niko couldn't help but admire, even though she maintained a stern posture.

"Nukka, we discussed this. Sled racing is too dangerous."

"Klondike and Miska and Nanuk are going, and

they're just pups." Nukka sat down stiffly. "Besides, I was better at dragline training than any of them, and you know it!"

Niko exhaled sharply. "True. But this is different. Sledding is tough work, and huskies are built to handle it. Cats aren't."

Nukka's head drooped a little. "I know I don't look like the rest of you. But I've trained, too. Don't I deserve a chance?"

Niko hesitated. The kitten looked so miserable at the thought of being left behind, she couldn't bear to disappoint her further. But there was simply no way Nukka could keep up with the pack on a run, much less pull a sled. And this was just training. What about the excursions Dad led, when the pack pulled the weight of several people through the woods for endless miles? Or the occasional rescue mission, when the huskies almost always ended up off the path and deep inside the woods, where more dangers awaited?

"I'm sorry, Nukka."

With that, Niko hurried off toward the sled.

She felt terrible crushing Nukka's spirits, but there was nothing else she could do. Because there was no way Niko would ever let the tiny kitten race with the pack.

They'd almost lost Nukka once. Niko would not risk the kitten's life again.

Chapter Twelve

NUKKA

Nukka sat on the porch, watching as Dad prepared the huskies for a run. She'd studied the team's different positions when she'd ridden in the sled with Mina. The huskies closest to the sled were the wheel dogs, and they were the biggest and strongest because they had to pull most of the weight. Most of the dogs in front of them were called team dogs, and today, they included the puppies. The swing dogs, like Suka, were close to the front. And of course, Niko was at the very front as the lead dog.

The huskies all wore harnesses attached to a series of thick lines that connected them to the sled. Nukka watched longingly as Dad stepped onto the sled's runners. He was bundled up in a thick coat with a giant hood pulled over his head so low that she couldn't even see his face when he yelled, *"Mush!"*

Instinctively, Nukka leaped up and off the porch at the command. The huskies surged forward, too, pulling the sled and Dad across the yard, heading for the path that led deep into the forest. Nukka ran after them, moving as fast as she could, but she couldn't keep up. Before she knew it, they'd vanished into the trees, and she was left alone.

Nukka eased to a halt, trying to catch her breath. She turned slowly and trudged back to the yard. Why was she made so differently from the rest of her family? She acted just like them, something that took a lot of practice and effort. She even looked like them … kind of. The color of their fur was similar, but her other features were different. Nukka was a cat, according to Niko. But Nukka didn't even really know what that meant.

"Psst."

Nukka froze. She sensed something nearby— not a husky, not a human. But something was watching her, and it was very, very close. Slowly, Nukka turned around.

Crouching in the grass just off the path was a creature with black-and-brown fur, pointy ears, and yellow eyes that seemed to glow. Nukka realized with a start that this was the creature who had been watching her train—the one hiding in the Fergusons' yard!

"Who are you?" Nukka stepped forward, the fur rising along her spine. "*What* are you?"

Slowly, the creature rose up on all fours, a languid, almost lazy movement. Behind her, a long tail just like Nukka's formed a curve like a question mark. "My name is Lola. And I'm a cat, honey—just like you."

Nukka stared at her in awe. Now that she was looking at this creature up close, Nukka couldn't deny the resemblance between them. She looked far more like Lola than she did Niko or the other huskies.

Lola crept forward, each paw landing noiselessly on the path. "I've been watching you a lot this last week, romping around with those dogs. Why are you pretending to be like them?"

"I'm not pretending." Nukka felt defensive as Lola circled her slowly, examining her from all angles. "They're my brothers and sisters. They're my pack."

"Oh, sweetie, no. You've got this all wrong." Lola's tail swished, and she bumped gently against Nukka's side. "But don't worry. I'm here to teach you how to be a cat."

She strolled back over to the tree and began rubbing her head against the trunk. Nukka eyed her nervously. Did she *want* to be a cat? What if that meant she wasn't part of the pack anymore?

More important, what in the world was Lola *doing* right now?

"I've got a little itch right behind my ear." Lola continued mashing her face against the bark, pressing her whole body against the tree. "One moment—ah, got it."

And then, a familiar sound reached Nukka's ears. It was a sound she herself still made, despite all of Klondike's teasing.

Purrrrrrrrr.

A strange rush of joy flooded Nukka. She leaped forward in delight. "I make that sound, too!"

"Well, of course you do." Satisfied, Lola stepped away from the tree. "You're a cat, sweetheart, just like I said. Or at least, you will be once I've taught you everything you need to know." She glared pointedly at Nukka's tail, which was wagging furiously. "Stop that."

Nukka forced herself to stop mid-wag. She sat absolutely still, mimicking Lola's posture.

"I'm ready. Teach me!"

As the week passed, Nukka quickly fell into a pattern. In the morning, she'd have breakfast with the pack, see Mina head off to school, and then watch as Dad strapped the huskies in and took them out for a tourist excursion or another training run. Watching her family sprint off across the snow without her didn't get any easier.

But while the pack was gone every morning, Nukka would have her lessons with Lola. And for a few hours, she would forget her hurt over being left out. Then the pack would return, exhausted and exhilarated, and Nukka would feel hurt all over again. She wanted so desperately to go with them, to race down the icy path with the wind in her face and her brothers and sisters all around her.

Still, Lola's lessons were a fun distraction. On Tuesday, she showed Nukka how to slink from room to room with just the right amount of elegance.

"It's more of a prowl, sweetheart." Lola glanced back at Nukka, who was following her around the Fergusons' living room, attempting to sway her back end. "There, that's more like it. No, stop wagging that tail! Now, watch and learn."

She headed down the hall to the office where Mrs. Ferguson worked during the day. Nukka followed, peeking around the door to watch as Lola jumped up onto the desk. Mrs. Ferguson's fingers flew over the keyboard; her brows were furrowed behind her glasses. To Nukka's surprise, Lola walked over the desk and *onto the keyboard*!

"Oh, Lola." Sighing, Mrs. Ferguson stroked the cat's back. Lola purred loudly, then went limp as her owner picked her up and placed her back on the floor. Undaunted, Lola jumped back on the desk. This time, she lay across the keyboard, mashing the keys down and purring louder than ever.

"Lola!" Mrs. Ferguson sounded more impatient now. She gently pushed Lola off the keyboard and tapped the keys frantically. "You just deleted an entire page!"

Lola responded by flicking her tail lazily, swatting Mrs. Ferguson's arm each time. Swat. Swat. Swat.

"Okay, I think it's time for a break." Mrs. Ferguson turned off the monitor and stood up, rubbing her temples. Nukka ducked out of sight as she left the office, then scurried inside. Lola leaped off the desk, her tail still swishing.

Nukka was bewildered. "Why did you do that?"

"Why?" Lola swaggered past Nukka. "Because I'm a cat, that's why."

On Wednesday, Lola taught Nukka how to hunt the tiny mice that lived in the Fergusons' shed. "Lie very still." Lola crouched low, her limbs folded beneath her body so that Nukka couldn't see so much as a toe. She mimicked the position.

"Now what?"

"Now wait."

Nearly an hour later, Lola yawned and stretched. "The mice are hiding today, apparently. Oh well."

Nukka tried to mask her relief. She didn't particularly relish the idea of chasing mice. She also thought that maybe Lola needed to work on her tracking skills. "What do you do if you catch one?"

Lola licked her front paw daintily. "Leave it on my owners' bed, usually."

"Why?" Nukka couldn't imagine leaving a mouse on Mina's bed.

"It's a gift, of course! It's only polite to share a successful hunt with your humans."

"Does your human like it?"

Lola's tail swished. "Oh yes. You should hear how loud she screams."

On Thursday, Lola taught Nukka to climb trees. Nukka tilted her head back, taking in the height of the tree. "That's *really* tall!"

"That's the point." Lola gazed up at the tree, too. "It's important that you learn to do this to protect yourself. Not many animals can climb trees—including dogs. Trees are the ideal hiding place."

Lola sprang onto the trunk, latching her claws onto the bark and beginning to climb. Nukka did the same, and her fear was soon replaced with joy. If only the pack could see her now! The next time she played a game of tag with Klondike, she wouldn't have to worry about outrunning him. She could just climb a tree and he'd never be able to reach her!

"Excellent." Lola perched on a thick branch, tail curled around her paws. Nukka sat next to her, gazing at the view. From here, she could see Mina's house *and* the Fergusons' house.

Lola's tail flicked slightly. "Tomorrow's lesson will be before the sun rises. Meet me on your back porch."

Nukka felt a little thrill at the thought of sneaking out. She barely slept that night, terrified that Niko or Mina would wake up and catch her. But when she crept out of her snug little bed, both the girl and the husky stayed fast asleep. Nukka scurried down the hall to the kitchen and darted through the doggie door. She blinked several times as her eyes adjusted to the total darkness outside.

"Over here." Lola's eyes glowed brighter than ever.

Nukka stared around in wonder. She'd never been out in the yard at night. Everything had a cool, greenish glow to it. "This is amazing!"

"Cats have far better nocturnal eyesight than dogs, you know." Lola lifted her head. "One of the many ways we're superior. Now, follow me."

Together, the cats slunk across the grass, heading for the Fergusons' house. Inside, Lola led Nukka to the bedroom. "Stay here by the door." Lola headed for the bed, tail held high. "Watch, and learn."

Nukka sat obediently, watching as Lola leaped silently onto the bed. Neither Mr. nor Mrs. Ferguson stirred—not until Lola let out the most mournful sound Nukka had ever heard.

"*Yowwwwl.*"

"Mmmph," Mrs. Ferguson mumbled into her pillow. "Stop it, Lola."

"Yowwwwwwwwwwwl."

"Not again," Mr. Ferguson groaned, pulling the blanket up over his head.

"YOWWWWWWWWWWWL!"

"Fine!" Mrs. Ferguson climbed off the bed and stood. Lola leaped off the bed and padded toward the door, a zombie-faced Mrs. Ferguson stumbling behind her. Nukka ducked back, watching as cat and owner made their way to the kitchen. When she peered around the corner, she saw Mrs. Ferguson dumping a can of cat food into a bowl. She set the bowl on the floor, and Lola sniffed at it for a few seconds. Then she walked to the other side of the kitchen and began grooming herself.

"Of course," Mrs. Ferguson muttered, heading back to her room. Nukka waited until the woman was gone before creeping into the kitchen.

"Why did you do that?"

Lola didn't look up from her grooming. "To get my breakfast."

"But you aren't eating it!"

"That's not the point." Lola lowered her leg and

gave Nukka a pointed glare. "And you need to stop asking *why*, sweetheart. Because the answer is always the same—because we're cats, and this is what we do. Got it?"

"Yes." Nukka ducked her head meekly. But inside, she still wasn't sure she was a cat. Of course, she obviously wasn't a husky, either.

So then what *was* she?

Chapter Thirteen

Mina

Niko greeted Mina in her usual frenzy when she got home from school on Friday. As she knelt down to hug the husky, she heard Mom half laughing, half groaning in the next room.

"Nukka, stop! Come on…how am I supposed to get any work done?"

Mina hurried into the living room with Niko. They found Mom sitting cross-legged on the couch, her laptop open in her lap. "What's going on?"

Instead of responding, Mom simply pointed down at her laptop. Mina walked around the sofa and burst out laughing. Nukka was sitting right in the middle of the keyboard, looking very pleased with herself.

"It's been like this all afternoon," Mom told Mina, shaking her head. "Watch." She picked the kitten up and set her on the floor, then started typing. But Nukka immediately hopped up onto the couch, crawled into Mom's lap, and slithered between her arms. On the screen, Mina could see dozens of random letters appear as the kitten's tiny paws pressed the keyboard buttons.

"What does she want?" Mina asked, still giggling as Mom scratched Nukka under her chin. Niko tilted her head, clearly baffled by the kitten's antics.

"Oh, nothing in particular. My cat used to do this kind of thing all the time. When I wanted to cuddle, she'd have none of it. But as soon as I started doing something else, she just *had* to have my full attention." Mom smiled as she picked the kitten up and handed her to Mina. "Maybe Nukka finally realized she's a cat, not a husky."

Mina gave Nukka a kiss on the head as she headed to her room, Niko trotting along next to her. "Do you know you're a kitty now?" she asked, holding Nukka up so they were eye to eye. The thought actually made her a little sad. It was so funny to watch Nukka act like a puppy. Mina always had new videos to show Emily and the others at lunch, and the whole table would shriek with laughter at the sight of the kitten chewing bones or frolicking with the husky pups, tail wagging and tongue lolling. The one of Nukka during dragline practice was the unanimous favorite so far.

"She's so clever!" Emily had said, staring in amazement at the video of the kitten racing around the yard, dragging the rawhide along behind her. "Did any of the other pups get it right on the first try?"

"Nope," Mina replied proudly. "Just Nukka."

Emily shook her head. "It's too bad she can't actually go on runs with the other huskies. She might not be as strong as they are, but she's definitely super smart."

"You have *got* to put this on Instagram," Fiona had added. She said the same thing pretty much every time she saw a Nukka video.

Mina set Nukka down on her bed, then headed over to her desk and opened her laptop. She stroked the top of Niko's head as the laptop powered on. Overall, her first week of adapting to the pack had been a big success. She'd sat with Emily and the F Twins during lunch every day since talking to them at the food court, and they'd all been really nice. Thanks to all the videos of Nukka, Mina hadn't found it too hard not to talk about ClockWork. She'd *thought* about them. A lot. But anytime someone would say something that would remind her about a funny selfie Gentry had posted (with a goat at his aunt's farm!) or an interview with Halo's hairstylist (who recommended eleven different brands of something called hair clay) or Lyric's latest food obsession (jalapeño marmalade, which sounded really weird but Mina was totally going to look for it at the next farmers' market), she would swallow her comment and try to think of a funny Nukka story to tell them instead.

Still scratching Niko's head with one hand, Mina opened her browser and logged in to her email, where she had one new message from ClockWork's official newsletter. When she saw the title, her entire body froze.

NEW CLOCKWORK SINGLE:
Watch the brand-new video for "Running Out" now!

"Omigosh!" Mina squealed so loud that Niko leaped up on all fours. "Niko, there's a new ClockWork video!" She opened the email and scrolled through all the text until she found the link, then clicked. A new page opened, and Mina's heart pounded as she turned the volume up all the way. The screen went black, then six silhouettes appeared against a bright purple background. Mina clapped both hands over her mouth to keep from squealing again as six voices sang in harmony.

> *"It won't stop-stop-stop*
> *You can't stop-stop-stop*
> *It won't stop-stop-stop because . . .*
> *You're running out of—"*

A fast, driving beat kicked in, blaring from the speakers. Mina leaped up and her chair toppled backward. Niko sprang up on all fours, tilted her head back, and howled as Mina jumped up and down in time with the beat. Normally, she'd be singing along with Niko, but she had to learn the words first. She usually managed to memorize all the lyrics by the fifth or sixth time she heard a new song.

When the video ended, Mina lunged for her laptop to hit REPLAY.

"What'd you think, Niko?" she asked breathlessly. The husky panted happily, clearly ready for another round of singing. "Nukka, how about you?"

Mina glanced over her shoulder, then did a double take. The kitten stood rigid on her bed, claws digging into the comforter. Her bright amber eyes were wide with alarm. Mina collapsed into giggles as the video started up again.

"Sorry, Nukka!" Mina said over the music, hurrying over to her bed. She scooped up the tense kitten and hugged her close as she danced. "Me and Niko kind of have a routine when there's a new ClockWork song. Niko sings, I dance, and we listen to it until Mom yells at me to give it a rest."

Nukka relaxed slightly, peering over Mina's arm and gazing at Niko. The husky squeezed her eyes closed, waiting until the voices came in before she started howling.

"It won't stop-stop-stop . . ."
"AROOOOO-ROOO-ROOO!"
"Mew! Mew! MEWWWWW!"

Laughter bubbled up in Mina's chest again. She set Nukka on the floor next to Niko and grabbed her phone off the dresser, swiping the camera on and tapping RECORD. The kitten mimicked the husky perfectly: Both sat on their haunches, noses in the air, their eyes slit like they were concentrating very hard, their mouths round as they howled—or mewed—along with the song.

"What in the world?" Mom appeared in the doorway, gaping at Niko and Nukka. Grinning, Mina waited until the song ended before closing her camera app and tapping PAUSE on the video.

"Mom, you should have seen Nukka the first time I played it," Mina said, barely able to suppress her giggles. "She was *so* freaked out. And then I played it again, and she copied Niko exactly!"

"This kitten, I swear." Mom was smiling as she knelt down to scratch both Niko and Nukka under their chins. "She's really something special."

"She is," Mina agreed. Her phone vibrated in her hand, and she glanced at the screen. Her heart leaped when she saw it was a text from Emily.

Hey! Want to see a movie tonight? A bunch of us are meeting at the theater at 6:30!

"Mom, can I go see a movie with Emily tonight?" Mina asked immediately.

Mom glanced up and smiled. "Of course!" She stood up, brushing her hands off on her jeans. "I'm so glad you two patched things up, hon."

"What?" Mina blinked. "We didn't have a fight, Mom."

"I know. But, well..." Mom shrugged. "Dad and I both noticed that you didn't spend much time with her over the summer. We figured something happened but you didn't want to talk about it. Which is fine!" she added quickly. "I'm just glad you're friends again."

Mina smiled weakly. "Yeah. Me too."

After Mom left her room, Mina started to type a response to Emily.

Yes, I'll be there!

But then she stopped before sending it, her thumb hovering over the screen.

Mom was right—something *had* happened between her and Emily. The problem was that Emily had never told Mina what that something *was*. Mina had only found out why Emily had stopped hanging out with her by accidentally eavesdropping on her other friends.

Now Emily seemed to want to be friends again. But not *best* friends, not the way they used to be. She invited Mina to sit with her at lunch or to go to the movies. But Faith and Fiona were always there, and all three of them always wore those matching cord necklaces, and Mina felt like she didn't quite belong. She had a nagging suspicion that if she asked Emily if she wanted to have a sleepover or go for a hike, just the two of them, Emily would come up with some excuse.

Mina sank down in her desk chair, still holding her phone. If she went to the movies tonight, she could show Emily and the F Twins her latest video of Nukka. But what about the ClockWork song playing in the background? Would Emily get annoyed? Would Faith and Fiona laugh at Mina? Would they sneak off to the bathroom with their other friends and make fun of Mina for being "totally obsessed"?

Suddenly, Mina didn't feel hurt and sad anymore—she felt irritated. Emily and her friends just loved the videos of Nukka behaving like a husky. Why did they love a cat for her quirky behavior, but when a girl had a quirk—like, for example, a passionate interest in what was objectively the greatest band in the world—they teased her? After all, everyone had quirks and interests and hobbies!

It wasn't fair that the only way Mina could hang out with the group was by not talking about something she loved so much.

Swiveling around in her chair, Mina looked at Nukka. She'd dragged a tiny rubber bone off her bed and was curled up next to Niko, happily chewing away. Mina couldn't help but smile. Nukka genuinely seemed to love bones and roughhousing and Dad's homemade dog food. She wasn't copying the huskies' behavior—she was being *herself.*

Mina wanted to be herself, too. And what herself wanted to do tonight was watch this ClockWork video on repeat. Maybe while sketching out a new shirt design.

She deleted her response to Emily and typed a new one. Thanks, but I have plans tonight. Next time! ☺ Then, without giving herself a chance to second-guess her decision, she tapped SEND.

A weird rush of emotions swept through her. Sadness, leftover hurt, and a little bit of that gnawing feeling that she was missing out. But she also felt relieved. And that wasn't how anyone should feel about not hanging out with their supposed friends.

Sighing, Mina put her phone down on her desk. She lowered the volume on her laptop, then started the ClockWork video again. Tapping her foot, she clicked back over to the email and scanned it quickly. She was about to close her email and click back to the video when very small text at the bottom of the newsletter caught her eye.

Don't forget to follow us on Instagram and share your thoughts about "RUNNING OUT"!

Mina clicked the link immediately, and a new page loaded. She opened the most recent Instagram post and scrolled through the comments. Reading them made her smile—there were so many ClockWork fans out there who were just as obsessed as Mina! She was about to click on the next post when one comment caught her eye.

@GentrysGirl001: Anyone have any good merch recs besides the official shop? I NEED MORE CLOCKWORK STUFF!!!!

Mina's eyes widened. She glanced over at the box next to her dresser. She hadn't gotten a single customer at the Fairbanks farmers' market. But maybe she'd just been looking for customers in the wrong place.

"Niko, I think I'm in business," Mina said, turning back to her laptop and grinning from ear to ear. "Mina's Original Designs just found a bigger market."

Chapter Fourteen

Niko

Mountains of glittering snow stretching out as far as she could see. A cloudless sky overhead. The icy path beneath her paws.

Niko raced faster than she ever had in her life. Behind her, she could hear the rest of her pack panting as their paws hit the ground, and farther back, the sound of a sled scraping against the snow. The air was blissfully frigid, and every few seconds, a snowflake melted on Niko's tongue. Joy surged through her, pushing her to run even faster. This was the perfect race. Nothing could go wrong now.

"Meow!"

Niko kept racing, but her eyes darted around

nervously. What was that? She didn't see anything but snow. Was it one of the huskies?

"*Meow!*"

The sound grew louder. There, under that bush up ahead! Niko slowed her pace, but she couldn't stop—the pack would barrel into her unless they heard the right command. *Whoa!* Niko thought, willing Dad to call it out. *Whoa!*

"*MEOW!*"

Niko veered off the path, bracing herself for the crash. But nothing happened. She spun around in the spot. The pack, the sled, they'd all vanished. It was just Niko standing alone in the snow next to a bush. She sniffed the ground anxiously, sticking her head beneath the bush, but there was nothing there. What in the world was going on? Alarmed, Niko started to run again.

"*MEEOOWWWW!*"

Niko's eyes flew open, and she found herself staring at Mina's desk chair. Her legs fell still—she'd been running in her sleep—but she still felt anxious. The snow, the wind, the sky . . . that had all just been a dream. But that sound . . .

"MEEEOOOWOWOWOWOW!"

Niko shot up off her bed at the same moment Mina bolted upright. "Nukka!" Mina gasped, and Niko leaped up onto Mina's bed, her tail sticking straight out behind her.

Nukka sat on Mina's legs, looking perfectly awake. She gazed beseechingly at Mina. *"Meow!"*

Mina rubbed her eyes and glanced at the clock on her night table. "It's four in the morning!" she said, stifling a yawn. "Go back to sleep, Nukka."

She flopped back onto her pillow. After a moment, Niko curled up at the foot of Mina's bed. But she didn't take her eyes off Nukka. The kitten waited until Mina's breathing had slowed. Then she walked across the comforter and climbed onto the pillow. Niko stared in disbelief as Nukka leaned in so that her nose was almost touching Mina's.

"MRROOOWWWWWWW!"

"Nukka!" Mina yelled, pulling her pillow out from under her head and placing it over her face. But Nukka was relentless.

"*MEOW! MRRROWWW!*"

Niko sat up stiffly and thumped her tail twice against the comforter. "What do you think you're doing?"

Nukka's eyes glowed bright gold. "I want breakfast!"

"We eat breakfast in the morning." Niko was completely bewildered. "You know that."

"I want it NOW!" Nukka took a deep breath. "*MEOW! MEOW! MEOW! MEOW! MEOW!*"

"Argh!" Mina threw off the pillow and climbed out of bed. "Fine!"

She picked Nukka up and marched out of the room. Niko hesitated, then leaped off the bed and followed them. In the kitchen, she watched as Mina spooned some of the homemade cat food Dad had prepared into a tiny bowl. She set it on the floor in front of Nukka, who sniffed at it. Then, to both Mina's and Niko's surprise, she walked across the kitchen, sat down, and began grooming herself.

"Nukka, are you kidding me?" Mina groaned.

Niko waited until Mina had gone back to her

bedroom, leaving the uneaten bowl of food on the floor. "Why didn't you eat it?"

Nukka looked extremely pleased with herself. "That's not the point!"

"The point?" Niko was more confused than ever. "Mina was up late on her computer. She needs her sleep. And you made her wake up to feed you!"

"Exactly." Nukka yawned hugely, almost toppling over. She trotted out of the kitchen, and Niko trailed behind her, still trying to understand what had just happened. Back in Mina's room, Nukka climbed onto her little bed and soon fell fast asleep. Niko curled up on her own bed, but she didn't feel sleepy anymore. What was wrong with Nukka?

Suddenly, Niko's fur stood on end. She sat up straight, barely managing to suppress the growl she could feel rising in her chest. Something was watching them. There, in the window, a pair of glowing eyes—Niko caught a quick flash of movement as Lola disappeared. Niko relaxed slightly, sinking back down into a more comfortable position. She didn't especially like the Fergusons' cat, but

Lola wasn't a threat. But why had she been watching them just now?

Then Niko thought about Nukka's odd behavior over the last week. Like the way she would walk across Mom's laptop when she was trying to work. Or how she'd taunted Klondike into chasing her, then raced up a tree and stared smugly down at the bewildered pup. Or the way she walked sometimes, swinging her rear end back and forth in an exaggerated way.

The very same way Lola walked.

Niko narrowed her eyes. Then, as quietly as possible, she stood and crept from Mina's room. She hurried down the hall to the kitchen and slipped through the doggie door. Standing on the porch, Niko stared around the yard. It was pitch-black outside, but she could sense the cat was still lurking nearby.

"Looking for me?"

Niko swiveled around, irritated that Lola had managed to sneak up behind her. The cat lay beneath the table, her legs tucked under her body so that they were completely hidden. She looked like a loaf of bread with eyes and ears.

"Hello, Lola." Niko sat stiffly, keeping her gaze locked on the cat. "Have you been spending time with Nukka lately?"

"Yes, as a matter of fact." Lola blinked once, very slowly. Niko was surprised; she'd expected the cat to deny it. "And you're welcome."

Niko tilted her head. "For what?"

"For teaching that poor thing how to be a cat. She's all mixed up, spending so much time with you dogs. She actually thinks she's one of you, you know."

"I know." Niko thought about the hurt in Nukka's eyes every time the pack set off on a training run, leaving her behind. She tried to ignore a stab of guilt. "She is part of my family, though. She's my responsibility, not yours."

Lola's tail flicked sharply. "Letting her think she's a dog is hardly responsible, Niko."

Niko felt her hackles rise. "I'm not. Nukka and I have discussed this. She knows she's a cat."

"And yet she still romps around, chasing sticks and chewing bones." Lola's eyes glowed extra bright. "She still wants to race. Did you know that, Niko? Because I watch her, when you all let that human strap you up so that you can drag him into the woods. She wants to go with you. And no cat in their right mind would ever want to do anything so ... demeaning." Lola paused, letting her words sink in. "Like I said, you should be thanking me. Once Nukka fully embraces being a cat, you won't have to worry about her doing anything foolish."

Standing abruptly, Niko took a menacing step forward. Lola shrank back, her eyes narrowing as Niko glared at her.

"Back off, Lola. Nukka isn't yours to *teach*."

With that, Niko turned and stalked into the kitchen. She made her way back to Mina's room and curled up on her bed. But she didn't sleep.

What bothered her most of all wasn't that Lola was teaching Nukka how to be a cat. It was that Lola was *right*. After all, Nukka *was* a cat, and she should behave like one. She shouldn't want to race like a husky. It was exactly what Niko had told Nukka.

Niko *should* be grateful to Lola. But all she felt was bitterness, and a strange sense of loss.

❄ ❄ ❄

"She's giving Nukka cat lessons?" Suka's ears flickered in amusement. "Perfect. It's about time Nukka realized she's not one of us."

"She *is* one of us." Niko felt a ripple of irritation pass through her. She and Suka sat together on the back porch, watching as the pups and Nukka tussled over a piece of old rope. "Nukka is part of this pack."

"Yes, I know." Suka sniffed. "But she isn't a husky, Niko, no matter how much she tries to behave like us. She can't race. She certainly can't come on rescue missions. It's better for everyone if she doesn't *want* to."

When Niko ignored this, Suka bumped gently against her side. "It's a good thing, Niko. Nukka needs to spend time with her own kind, too."

The porch shook slightly beneath their feet as Kodiak lumbered toward them. "What's going on?"

Suka nodded at Nukka and the pups. "Lola next door has been teaching Nukka how to act like a cat. Not that you can tell right now."

"Good." Kodiak gave himself a shake, starting with his head and moving down to his tail. "You can't be something you're not. I can act like a cat, but that will never make me a cat."

Niko snorted. "You have no idea how to act like a cat."

"Is that so?" Kodiak stretched his front paws out, sticking his rump in the air. Then he started rubbing his side against one of the patio table's legs so hard, he actually lifted the table a few inches off the ground. It fell back down with a loud thump just as Dad stepped outside.

"Everything okay out here?" He peered at Kodiak, who stared back at him innocently. Finally, Dad shrugged and headed to the shed.

Suka's eyes sparkled with amusement. "I doubt many cats could lift a table like that."

"My point, exactly." Kodiak settled down on the patio, his tail curling around his back legs. "Nukka can act like a husky all she wants. But can she pull a sled? Can she race for hundreds of miles?"

"Of course not." Niko gazed out at Nukka, who was in the middle of a game of tug-of-war with Miska. She knew the tiny kitten wasn't built for the kind of racing huskies did. And besides, cats didn't have packs like dogs. Lola was the perfect example. She was independent, sneaking around in the dead of night alone, looking out for herself and no one else. That was simply the way cats were. They liked being alone.

But this pack was all Nukka had ever known. And when Niko pictured Nukka the way she'd looked when they'd found her under that bush, she couldn't help but think that being alone was the last thing Nukka needed.

Chapter Fifteen

NUKKA

Nukka gnawed on the old rope, keeping one eye on the Fergusons' yard. Miska had given up the game of tug-of-war when Klondike had emerged from the bushes with a gigantic stick clamped between his teeth. Nukka had almost raced after them, but they'd been playing hard for almost an hour and she had to admit she was tired.

And she wasn't the only one. Mina had yawned all through breakfast, and Nukka couldn't help noticing her eyes were kind of red. Her pride over her outstanding catlike performance in the middle of the night had quickly been replaced with guilt. Especially when she'd watched Mina pick up her little bowl and dump her uneaten food in the trash.

Why did *I do that?* Nukka wondered. Then she reminded herself of what Lola had told her: *Because we're cats, and this is what we do.*

Nukka glanced over at the Fergusons' yard again, but there was no sign of Lola. Although that didn't mean she wasn't lurking around nearby, watching. Nukka suspected none of the huskies knew just how often the neighbor's cat spied on their antics.

"Toys! Toys! Toys!" Klondike, Miska, and Nanuk hurtled toward the shed in a frenzy of yapping as Dad emerged, carrying an armload of pipes, tubes, and cones. Nukka leaped up and sprinted over to join them.

"Whoa there, guys!" Dad laughed, almost losing his balance as Nukka and the pups raced around him in circles. "Glad you're excited, but it's going to take me a while to set all of this up."

"Can I help?" Mina had appeared on the porch, and Nukka was relieved to see she looked much more awake now. She scampered over to greet her and felt a rush of joy when Mina picked her up and kissed her on the head.

"Sure, hon," Dad replied, sticking one of the shorter pipes into a hole at the end of the longest pipe. "But I thought you were going to spend the day working on new T-shirt designs?"

"I can do that later." Mina scratched Nukka under the chin as she walked across the grass to join Dad. "Actually, I was wondering if you could help me."

Dad glanced up. "I'm pretty crummy at design, sweetie."

Mina laughed. "No, not that. I, um . . . I think I want to expand my business."

"Oh?"

Nodding, Mina set Nukka down on the grass and helped Dad fit more of the short pipes into the long one. The grass tickled Nukka's backside, and she shifted, trying to scratch the itch. The pups settled on the grass next to Dad, watching with curious eyes as he worked.

"I want to sell my T-shirts online," Mina continued. Her words came out in a rush, and Nukka realized she was nervous. "There are *so* many ClockWork fans on Instagram, and I want to create an account for Mina's Original Designs. I just think it makes a lot more sense to sell them online instead of at the farmer's market. I mean, there aren't that many ClockWork fans in Fairbanks, and—"

"Mina, hon." Smiling, Dad held up a hand. "I think that's a *great* idea, and I'd be happy to help you with it. After all, you're always a huge help to my business."

"Really?" Mina beamed. "Thanks, Dad!"

Still unable to reach the itch, Nukka gave up on scratching and stood. As she began rubbing her backside against one of the poles, she heard herself start to purr. All the pups turned to stare at her, ears perked up.

"Hey, that husky pup sounds an awful lot like a kitten!" Dad joked.

Mina giggled. "Mom said she's been acting more like a cat lately. She actually woke me up in the middle of the night, meowing!"

"Really?" Dad looked down at Nukka, who stopped rubbing against the pole and gazed back at him. She wasn't sure whether to feel proud or ashamed. "What did she want?"

"I thought maybe she was hungry," Mina said, fitting the last short pipe into the long one. "She followed me into the kitchen, but when I put her food bowl down, she wouldn't touch it."

"She ate all her breakfast this morning, though, right?"

"Yup." Mina tickled Nukka under the chin. "She was just being a silly kitty."

Klondike tilted his head. "Silly kitty!"

"I am not." Nukka glared at him.

"You aren't what?" Klondike's ears flattened against his head. "Silly? Or a kitty?"

"Stop saying that!"

"Silly kitty! Silly kitty! Silly kitty!"

"Stop it!" Nukka pounced on the pup, who rolled onto his back and tossed her off easily. It seemed like every day, all the husky pups got a little bit bigger and a little bit stronger, while Nukka stayed the same. Well, that wasn't entirely true. Nukka knew she was growing, too. She was much stronger than she had been when Niko and Mina had found her. Besides, sometimes her smaller size gave her an advantage.

She waited until Klondike was back on all fours, then leaped onto his back. Klondike spun around and around trying to reach her, but Nukka clung to his fur and stayed just out of range of his teeth. "Who's silly now?"

"Okay, Nukka," Dad said, laughing. "That's enough!" Obediently, Nukka hopped off Klondike's back and scampered to the porch, where the older huskies were watching the pups. Nukka cozied up next to Niko, just in case Klondike decided to come after her, but he was already distracted with one of the pipes strewn over the grass.

The pipes Mina and Dad had been fitting together looked like a giant comb. Nukka watched intently as they lifted it together so that the shorter pipes stuck straight up in the air. "What are they doing with those toys?"

Suka settled down on her other side, crossing her paws delicately. "Those aren't toys. They're building an obstacle course."

"It's part of our training," Niko added. "To improve agility. During a race, the terrain isn't always a straight path. There are hills, fallen trees, bumps, cracks—it can be very dangerous."

Nukka felt a twinge of annoyance. It seemed like Niko was constantly pointing out how dangerous racing was—but only to Nukka. What about how *fun* racing was? Because clearly all the huskies—especially Niko—absolutely loved it.

When Dad and Mina finished setting up the obstacle course, the yard looked like a maze of pipes and poles, tunnels and cones, ramps and hoops. Mina jogged over to the edge of the yard, herding the husky pups with her. Dad let out a short whistle, and Suka leaped off the porch and bounded over to him.

"What's she doing?" Nukka wondered aloud.

Niko sat up straight. "She's going to run through the course. Suka is excellent at obstacle courses—watch closely!"

Nukka sat up, too, her gaze fixed on the snow-white husky. She stood perfectly still at Dad's side, facing the opening of one of the tunnels.

"Are you recording?" Dad called to Mina, and she gave him the thumbs-up. "Okay, Suka—let's go!"

Suka took off like a shot into the tunnel. She burst out the other side and raced up one of the ramps, across a platform, then back down another ramp. Then she reached the pipes sticking up like a comb and weaved through them, darting left, right, left, right, at a speed that made Nukka dizzy. Dad jogged from one obstacle to the next as Suka leaped over a series of increasingly high bars, zoomed through a curved tunnel, then sprinted toward the last obstacle—a steep ramp with no platform on the other side. Nukka's fur stood on end as Suka charged up the ramp. Was she going to jump off it from that height? But when Suka reached the center of the ramp, the end that was touching the ground began to lift up, and the end that was sticking up lowered. Nukka realized the husky's weight had shifted the balance, and she watched in astonishment as Suka sped down the ramp while it lowered safely to the ground.

Dad was looking at his watch. "Forty-six seconds!" he exclaimed, beaming. "Good girl, Suka!" He tossed the white husky a treat, which she caught easily, tail swaying high in the air.

"See what I mean?" Niko seemed proud, and Nukka understood why. Suka had made the obstacle course look easy. Actually, she'd made it look *fun*. Nukka was itching to try it herself, but she had a feeling Niko wouldn't like that very much.

"Kodiak!" Dad called. "Want to give it a go?"

Behind Niko and Nukka, the giant husky rose slowly and yawned before ambling over to Dad.

For the next hour, Nukka watched as, one by one, the huskies completed the obstacle course. While Suka was by far the fastest, each husky had his or her own strong points. Kodiak's large size made weaving through the poles more difficult for him, but his strength made him a powerful jumper. Sakari hesitated in front of each tunnel, but her side-to-side weaving was even more nimble than Suka's. Niko was fearless and sure-footed, moving from one obstacle to the next without any urging from Dad.

"We get to do this tomorrow." Klondike had joined Nukka on the porch, tail thumping loudly against the table leg. "Kodiak told me."

"Really?" Nukka felt a bolt of excitement. "I can't wait!"

"Not you, silly kitty!" Klondike gave Nukka a smug look. "This is part of husky training."

Nukka was undaunted. "Like the dragline? Because Dad let me do that! And unlike you, I did it right on the first try."

Klondike narrowed his eyes. "I bet I can do the obstacle course faster than you. I bet you can't even *finish* it."

"Oh, yeah?"

"Yeah!"

"Lunchtime!" Dad called, leading the huskies back to the porch. "Come on, guys."

"That was awesome," Mina said as she followed him back into the house. "I can't wait for the pups to try it!"

Klondike gave Nukka a pointed look. "The *pups*. Not the silly kitties."

"I'm a husky!"

"You are not!"

"I am so, and I'll prove it!" Nukka had had

enough of everyone telling her what she was and what she wasn't. "I'll do the obstacle course. I'll do it faster and better than you!"

"Right now?" Klondike stood eagerly, tail wagging.

Nukka glanced at the open door to the kitchen, where she could hear Dad preparing lunch for the pack. If she and Klondike tried to run the obstacle course now and Dad caught them, they might get into trouble. Then she imagined Lola lurking outside Mina's bedroom window and had an idea.

"No. Let's race tonight."

❄ ❄ ❄

Nukka felt excited and anxious for the rest of the day. She and Klondike had told the other pups about their bet, and they'd all agreed to keep it secret from the rest of the pack. After all, they knew Niko would never approve of them sneaking outside at night. Which, Nukka had to admit, made the whole thing even more exciting.

That night, Mina sat behind the glow of her laptop for what felt like hours. Nukka stayed in her bed, gnawing on her bone and doing her best to look completely innocent. Every once in a while, she cast a glance at Niko to see if the husky seemed at all suspicious. But Niko was busy with a piece of rawhide Mom had given her after dinner.

At last, Mina closed her laptop. "Night, Nukka," she said. "Night, Niko." She flipped off the light switch and climbed into bed.

Nukka waited until Mina's breathing turned deep and slow. She stood slowly, keeping her eyes on Niko, and crept toward the door.

Once Nukka was out in the hall, she raced silently to the living room. Sakari was snoring peacefully on her bed next to the sofa, her pups all curled up at her side. When she saw them, Nukka felt a momentary pang of sadness—and doubt. Maybe Klondike was right. Maybe Nukka needed to accept the fact that she wasn't a husky, no matter how much she felt like one.

Klondike opened one eye and spotted her. He slid out from beneath Sakari's paw, waking Miska and Nanuk as he did. The pups climbed out of the bed with surprising stealth, and Sakari didn't even stir.

Nukka was impressed. "So sneaky. Maybe *you're* the silly kitties!"

"Very funny." Klondike bumped against her in a friendly way as the four of them headed to the kitchen, and Nukka's doubt vanished. She might not look like the pups, but they were still her siblings. And besides, Nukka had been the best of all of them at dragline racing. She would conquer this obstacle course, too.

One by one, the pups and Nukka clambered through the doggie door and out onto the porch. Nukka's eyes adjusted immediately, and at the sight of the tunnels and pipes and cones, her heart started to beat fast with excitement.

"Let's go!" Klondike raced toward the first tunnel, Nukka, Miska, and Nanuk on his heels. The four of them stopped at the opening, and Klondike took a step back. "Whoa. That's really, really dark."

Nukka had to admit he was right. It was a scary

sort of dark, a total pitch blackness she'd never seen before.

Miska tucked her tail. "Maybe this isn't such a good idea."

"You could skip the tunnel." Nanuk tilted his head, looking from Nukka to Klondike. "Let's go run up the ramps instead!"

Klondike actually seemed to be considering this. But Nukka moved forward, gazing at the tunnel. Her eyes had adjusted to the dark, and now she could see it wasn't *totally* black inside. In fact, the longer she stared, the more Nukka could see a greenish-gray circle of dim light at the end. She remembered how Niko had tackled each obstacle fearlessly. If racing was dangerous, then it was important for huskies to be fearless. Nukka decided right then and there that she could be fearless, too.

"You can chicken out if you want, but I'm doing the whole thing."

With that, Nukka launched forward into the tunnel. She heard a high-pitched bark behind her, and then the unmistakable sound of Klondike racing after her. Nukka flew out of the tunnel and sped up a ramp, across the platform, and down another ramp. She spotted the giant comb like thing and put on a burst of speed, darting from side to side just like Suka had, putting distance between herself and Klondike. Nukka's heart raced with excitement as she sprinted for the bars. Her smaller size was actually an advantage! And after the darkness of the tunnel, the rest of the obstacle course seemed positively bright. Nukka leaped over the bars and heard another bark behind her. Klondike was catching up to her, but Nukka was almost finished with the course. She spotted the last, extra-steep ramp and tore straight up . . .

Then stopped at the top.

Nukka's eyes darted here and there, her front paws clinging to the edge of the ramp. "It's supposed to drop to the ground!"

Miska and Nanuk scurried across the grass and stopped right below to stare up at her.

"You're too light!" Miska looked worried. "You don't weigh enough to push the ramp down!"

Nanuk's tail wagged frantically. "Better look out—Klondike is right behind you!"

Behind Nukka, the sound of paws pounding against the grass grew louder and louder. Then the ramp wiggled as Klondike charged up to the top. When he reached the middle, the ramp jerked forward, and suddenly the ground was speeding closer and closer!

Miska and Nanuk darted out of the way as the end of the ramp fell. Nukka waited until Klondike had almost reached her, and then she jumped as far as she could.

She landed lightly on the grass. A second later, Klondike tumbled off the ramp and rolled a few feet away from her. Nukka, Miska, and Nanuk hurried over to him.

"Are you okay?" Miska sniffed her brother, concerned. But Nukka could see his tail was wagging, and sure enough, he popped up quickly and shook himself off.

"Who won?" Klondike looked from Miska to Nanuk, his eyes bright.

"I did!" Nukka lifted her head proudly. "I landed before you did!"

"Aw." Klondike's disappointment only lasted a second. "Well, you had a head start."

"Only because I wasn't scared of the tunnel!"

"I wasn't scared!"

"Yes, you were!"

"No, I—"

Suddenly, the porch lights blared on. Nukka and the pups whirled around as the back door flew open. Mina stood there, squinting out into the yard.

"Nukka? Klondike?"

The fear and worry in her voice tugged at Nukka's heart. She realized Mina couldn't see them, and she hurried toward the porch, the pups right behind her.

Then Niko appeared at Mina's side, her light blue eyes going straight to Nukka, and Nukka realized she was in very, very big trouble.

Chapter Sixteen

Niko

Niko stood stiffly at Mina's side. Behind her, Sakari suddenly hurtled out the back door and toward the pups with a sharp yip.

"Mina, hon, what on earth..." Mom and Dad stepped onto the porch, both wearing their pajamas. Niko remained absolutely still as Mina scooped Nukka up and turned around.

"Hey, what are you guys doing out here?" Dad stepped aside, allowing Sakari to herd her pups back into the house. "Mina, you didn't let them out, did you?"

"Of course not!" Mina cuddled Nukka close to her chest. "Niko woke me up a few minutes ago because Nukka was gone. We looked all over the house and saw the pups weren't with Sakari anymore."

"So they all came out here?" Mom asked in disbelief. "Why would they do that?"

Mina hesitated. "Okay, this is going to sound really out there, but when I got to the kitchen, I looked out the window. And maybe my eyes were playing tricks on me, but I think...I think they were trying to do the obstacle course!"

Niko's head jerked up. She stared at Nukka, who tucked her head under the crook of Mina's arm.

"Nukka was on top of the last ramp," Mina went on, pointing. "And then one of the pups, I think it was Klondike, he started running up, too. That's when I called Niko and we came outside."

Mom started to respond, then squinted out at the yard. "Well, looks like you found them just in time. It's starting to snow!"

Everyone turned to gaze at the thick, fat snowflakes falling from the sky. Niko could sense in her bones that this was the *big* snow, the one that would cover the ground in a thick white blanket for the next several months. Normally, she'd be thrilled. But right now, she was too upset for even a single tail wag.

"What are we doing standing out here in our pj's?" Dad said suddenly, stamping his feet and rubbing his arms. "Let's go inside!"

Niko followed the family back into the kitchen. Mina still hadn't put Nukka down, and Niko suspected the girl was as worried as she was about Nukka's middle-of-the-night adventure.

"Nukka, you silly kitty," Mina crooned, nuzzling the kitten with her nose. "What were you thinking?"

Niko stared expectantly at Nukka, who still wouldn't meet her gaze. *Yes, Nukka. What* were *you thinking?*

The next morning after breakfast, Dad took the huskies out onto the porch. He let out a low whistle at the sight of the yard.

"Two feet at least!" he called into the kitchen, where Mom was cleaning the dishes. "And it's still coming down. Maybe now I'll get some more folks signed up for excursions! This season's been too light so far."

He pulled on his rubber boots and made his way to the obstacle course to clear the snow off the ramps. As he worked, Niko and Sakari rounded up the pups and Nukka. Usually, they were full of energy right after breakfast. But this morning, everyone seemed subdued—even Klondike, who yawned so widely Niko could see every one of his tiny, sharp teeth.

"Tired?" Niko cocked her head at him, and he stared at his paws contritely. "Sneaking outside in the middle of the night was foolish for many reasons. You're lucky this snowstorm didn't start while you were out there—it could have buried you!"

Sakari snapped her jaw lightly. "There are predators in the woods who hunt at night."

"And the temperatures are much colder." Niko looked pointedly at Nukka. "You could easily freeze to death. What you did was very dangerous!"

To her surprise, Nukka stared back at her defiantly. "You think everything is dangerous!"

Niko stiffened. Around her, the pack fell completely still and silent. All eyes were on the tiny kitten daring to challenge their leader.

Standing slowly, Niko took a step closer to Nukka. "There are a lot of dangers out there. Part of training to be a sled dog is learning how to deal with those dangers during a race."

"But racing is fun, too!" Nukka's tail curled defensively around her paws. "I only snuck out because you won't even let me train on the obstacle course. I deserve a chance to prove myself—and I did!"

Klondike thumped his tail against the porch, and Niko glanced at him. "Nukka's right. She did the whole obstacle course. She even beat me!"

"And she ran right into the tunnel," Miska added eagerly. "It was so dark that the rest of us were scared, but Nukka wasn't! She was really brave!"

Nukka sat up straighter, and for a split second, Niko felt a rush of pride for the kitten. But that was quickly replaced with an intense fear.

"What you did last night was not brave." Niko stared at each pup in turn, her eyes falling on Nukka last. "It was foolish. You could have been hurt. Nukka, you should have known better after what you went through when we found you!"

Nukka let out an angry mew. "It's not fair! You think I'm still weak, but I'm not—I can race! I proved it!"

"No." Niko leaned closer, and Nukka cowered. "What you proved last night is that you are reckless and I can't trust you. *That* is why you'll never race with us, Nukka."

With that, Niko turned and headed back into the kitchen, ignoring the stares of the rest of the pack. She headed straight for Mina's bedroom, but Suka caught up with her in the hall. Mina's door was open just a crack, and Niko could see her sitting behind her laptop, still in her pajamas.

"That was harsh." Suka's light blue eyes fixed unblinkingly on Niko, who dipped her head.

"It was necessary."

"I suppose." Suka gave her ears a little flick. "You know this means Nukka will probably start spending more time with that cat."

Niko ignored a twinge of hurt. "Maybe that's for the best. Nukka is a cat, after all."

With that, she nosed the door open wider and headed straight for Mina's bed. Niko leaped onto the pillows, turned around a few times, then settled down. She gazed at Mina, trying not to think about how hurt and defiant Nukka had looked outside. Niko couldn't help but admire the kitten's determination. But every time she thought about Nukka racing across the snow, or sneaking out at night, or crawling through pitch-black tunnels, she remembered the moment when Dr. Li had told them Nukka might not survive. Niko and Mina had made a vow right there to do everything they could to save the kitten's life. She couldn't risk Nukka getting hurt like that again, no matter how much she wanted to race with the pack.

"Niko!" Mina looked up from her laptop and blinked. "I didn't even hear you sneak in." She glanced at the clock on her night table. "I guess I should have breakfast, huh? Just a few more minutes..."

She turned back to the screen, her fingers flying over the keyboard. Niko rested her head on her paws and watched. It seemed like Mina spent all her free time on her laptop and phone lately; she hadn't been out with Emily this weekend. But the sadness that had clung to Mina the whole summer was gone. She smiled as she typed, and she giggled every time she checked her phone, as if it had told her a joke.

Mina had always struck Niko as being more dog than cat. But maybe she liked being on her own more than Niko thought. Closing her eyes, Niko sighed.

If Mina could find a way to be happy without being part of a pack, maybe Nukka could, too. At least then she would be safe.

Chapter Seventeen

Mina

Mina wiggled in her chair as she scrolled through her Instagram feed. In the last week, she'd spent every spare minute after school working on her business. On Monday, Dad had set up a website for Mina's Original Designs, while Mom had helped her out with a photo shoot so that Mina had a picture of herself modeling each of her shirts. She'd posted the photos, along with the digital images of her artwork, on Instagram on Tuesday, along with a link to her website. On Wednesday, she woke up to over one hundred comments raving about her designs. By Thursday, she had fifty-one orders.

Fifty-one! At ten dollars a shirt, that came out to $510! Of course, a lot of that went to buying more silk-screening supplies and plain T-shirts. But even after that, Mina would have over $300 in profit. And the orders were still coming in!

On Friday during lunch, Mina sat alone at the end of a table and pulled out her sketch pad. She'd been chatting with a few of her new Instagram followers that morning, and @GentrysGirl001 (her real name was Hallie) had pointed out that Gentry's selfie with the goat had almost one thousand comments and over ten thousand likes.

@GentrysGirl001: You should do a goat shirt! 😎
@RachelLuvsHalo: OMG YES 😂😂😂
@Lyricallee: ok I would SO buy that shirt
@MinasOriginalDesigns: LOL ok
@GentrysGirl001: Wait really??
@MinasOriginalDesigns: Yes!!

Mina sketched quickly, pencil flying across the paper. Another Instagram comment had joked about the goat being an honorary member of ClockWork, which gave Mina an idea. First, she sketched the silhouettes of the six members exactly like they appeared at the beginning of the new "Running Out" video. Then she added the silhouette of a goat on the far left, standing on his hind legs and striking a pose. As she drew, Mina brainstormed different names for the design. The Seventh Member, maybe? No—Running Out of Goats! Perfect.

"Hey, Mina!" Emily sat down across from Mina and set down her lunch tray. Mina glanced up in surprise as Fiona and Faith joined her, too. "What's that?"

Mina held her arm protectively over her drawing. "Oh, it's . . ." She paused. *Nothing*. She'd almost said her design was nothing. But her designs weren't nothing, and neither was her business, which was doing very well, thank you very much. Suddenly, Mina realized she was tired of being ashamed of her ClockWork obsession. If Fiona and Faith laughed at her, so what?

"It's an idea for a new ClockWork T-shirt," Mina told Emily, ignoring the amused look that passed between the F Twins. "I've been selling them online, and this morning someone requested this design."

She waited, expecting Emily to look annoyed at the mention of ClockWork. But Emily actually seemed interested.

"You're selling them online?"

"Yeah." Mina went back to her sketch. "My dad set up a website, and I've been posting about them on Instagram."

"How many have you sold?" Faith asked, taking a bite of her apple.

"Fifty-one."

"Whoa!" Emily exclaimed, and even the F Twins looked impressed. "That's amazing!"

"Thanks!" Mina smiled, then chewed her lip. "Actually, I'm a little nervous. I mean, I have to silk-screen them all by hand. It takes a lot of time. And I think this new one might be really popular. What if I can't keep up with the orders?"

To her surprise, Fiona leaned forward, her eyes sparkling with excitement. "Then you call this design a *limited edition*."

"What?"

"Oh, yeah!" Faith said eagerly. "Make, like, twenty of them, and that's it. Then you put it on the website and say it's a limited edition design, only twenty available."

"And you charge a lot more for them," Fiona added, sitting back with a satisfied expression.

Mina looked from one girl to the other. They both seemed totally sincere.

"That's a really good idea," she admitted. "How do you guys know so much about running an online business?"

Emily fingered her cord necklace with the little unicorn charm. "Faith's mom sells her jewelry online."

"We help her out a lot," Faith added. "These necklaces are so easy to make."

"And we help her with shipping, too," Fiona said. "Every Friday night, we watch movies and wrap up that week's orders to mail. It's fun!"

"We could help you!" Emily said, smiling at Mina. "I don't know anything about silk screening, but..."

"It's easy!" Mina replied quickly. "I could show

you. It would be really great to have some help. Maybe tomorrow, at my house?"

"Great!" Emily looked from Fiona to Faith. "Are you guys in?"

"Definitely!" Fiona said.

Faith nodded, her mouth full of sandwich. "Have you posted any videos of Nukka on Instagram yet?" she asked once she'd swallowed. "I know she doesn't have anything to do with your business, but seriously—you'd get, like, a *ton* of followers. Everyone loves kittens."

"I haven't yet, but I will," Mina said eagerly. "I'll post about her tonight!"

Mina spent the rest of the day practically bubbling over with happiness. When she got home from school, Niko greeted her at the door enthusiastically.

"Hey, girl!" Mina knelt down to hug Niko around the neck. "Where's Nukka?"

Niko stepped back, and Mina got to her feet. She followed the husky into the living room, where the pups were gnawing at tiny rawhide bones.

Finally, Mina spotted the kitten sitting on the windowsill, staring out at the snow.

"Nukka?" Mina walked over, concerned. Nukka had been unusually subdued ever since Mina and Niko had caught her and the pups in the yard in the middle of the night. When Nukka saw Mina, her tail thumped against the windowsill a few times. For a moment, Mina thought the kitten was about to spring off the sill and run toward her, the way she normally did when Mina got home from school. But then Nukka turned away again.

Frowning, Mina picked the kitten up. "Aw, Nukka. What's wrong?" The kitten nuzzled against her chest and began to purr when Mina scratched her behind the ears. "Come on. I know what'll cheer you up."

She carried Nukka to her room, calling hello to Mom, who was in the kitchen making a big pot of venison chili. Mina set Nukka down on her bed, waiting for Niko to come inside before closing her door.

"Ready, guys?" Mina bent over her laptop, opened the "Running Out" video, and hit PLAY.

"It won't stop-stop-stop...
You can't stop-stop-stop..."
"AROOOOO-ROOO-ROOO!"
"Mew! Mew! MEWWWWW!"

After listening to the song at least a hundred times, Mina had every word committed to memory. She sang along with Niko and Nukka, pulling her sketch pad out of her backpack and flipping to the goat design. The sketch was complete; now Mina had to add color.

When the song finished, Mina hit REPEAT. And then again, and again. Outside her window, the snow was falling heavily once more, adding to the heaps of snow that had been piling higher and higher all week. Niko and Nukka stopped singing along after the second round, curling up on their respective beds and dozing off while Mina continued to work. She couldn't wait to show Hallie and her other followers how the goat design had turned out.

After more than an hour of painting, Mina's stomach started to rumble. She set her brushes down, stood up, and stretched just as the doorbell rang three times very fast, followed by a loud knock-knock-knock. Niko's head jerked up, and Mina frowned. Who would be visiting them in the middle of a snowstorm?

Mina hurried down the hall, Niko right behind her. They reached the foyer just as Dad pulled the front door open.

"Jack!" Dad said in surprise. "Good to see you. Come on in!"

"Thanks, Logan." Trooper Jack stamped the snow off his boots before stepping inside. His expression was grim, and Mina's stomach dropped. She knew what that look meant.

"I hate to bother you," Trooper Jack began. "But I've got a bit of a situation. An expedition group lost a man twelve hours ago. We've had folks out looking, but no luck so far, and now that the sun's down it's only going to get harder to find him."

Dad was already opening the front closet and pulling out his boots. "Say no more, Jack. Just give me fifteen minutes to prepare the sled."

Trooper Jack let out a sigh of relief. "Thanks a bunch, Logan. I'll radio you the coordinates for the location."

With that, he headed back into the snowy night. Dad turned to Mina, who swallowed hard.

"Ready for our first rescue mission of the season?" he asked, and Mina nodded firmly. Dad smiled. "Meet me out back when you're dressed."

"Okay." Mina watched as Niko followed Dad outside. When she turned around, she was surprised to see Nukka sitting behind her, eyes wide with curiosity.

Leaning over, Mina gave Nukka a little scratch under the chin.

"*Second* rescue mission of the season," she whispered. "You were the first." The kitten blinked up at her, and Mina remembered finding her under that bush, exhausted and starving and cold. The memory filled her with resolve, and she hurried to her room to get ready.

Somewhere out in the wilderness, a hiker was lost. He could be trapped or injured, and with the temperature dropping as night fell—not to mention the bears and wolves—he might not last too much longer. That meant it was time for Mina and her dad to do what they did best: pack up the sled, strap up the huskies, and rescue this hiker before it was too late.

Chapter Eighteen

NUKKA

Nukka sat perfectly still as Mina pulled on her coat and boots. Someone was lost and freezing and starving, just like she had been. A distant, bleary memory surfaced in her mind: the roar of a passing truck, Niko's wet snout, Mina carrying the blanket, Dad lifting her up ever so gently...

The pack was going on a rescue mission. It would be dangerous, Nukka knew, but she wasn't afraid. This was it—her chance to prove herself once and for all!

She leaped up and followed Mina down the hall and into the kitchen. The back door was wide-open, and the temperature inside was dropping quickly. Nukka slipped past Mom, who was busy filling thermoses with hot tea, and stepped out onto the porch.

Niko and the other huskies were busy eating a quick dinner, while Mina and Dad put on hats and scarves. Then they started wading to the shed to pull out the sled.

"Wish we could go." Klondike appeared at Nukka's side. "It's really dark out there, though."

But Nukka wasn't looking at the huskies anymore. A pair of glowing yellow eyes were visible beneath the table, fixed on Nukka.

All week, Nukka had been avoiding Lola. The obstacle course had changed everything. Nukka knew she was a cat—but she'd finished that course in the dark. She'd even beaten Klondike! And most important, she'd *loved* it. She wanted to race; she wanted to help pull the sled; she wanted to go on this rescue mission. Didn't that make her a husky in her heart?

After a few minutes, Klondike scurried back inside the warm house. But Nukka stayed where she was, watching the preparations. Dad was busy tightening knots and securing the lines that would connect the huskies' harnesses to the sled. Mina was strapping each husky into his or her harness, checking every buckle twice. Mom bustled back and forth from the kitchen to the sled, each time carrying another armload of supplies. Nukka was amazed at how much weight the pack would be pulling. No wonder Dad trained the pups so much!

When the huskies were all strapped up, Nukka ducked back into the kitchen. She leaped up onto the counter where Dad kept the pups' leashes and harnesses, clamped her teeth around her harness, and jumped back down. Nukka raced across the porch and into the yard. The snow was hard-packed by now, and her paws only sank a tiny bit. She reached Mina, dropped her harness, and—

"MEOW! MEOW! MEOWWW!"

"Nukka!" Mina bent down and picked up the kitten. Then she spotted the harness at her feet. "Dad, look!" she called, and Dad turned around. "Nukka brought her harness out. She wants to come!"

Dad's scarf hid his mouth, but Nukka could tell from the twinkle in his eyes that he was smiling. "Sorry, Nukka. I'm afraid this isn't safe for kittens!"

Nukka squirmed and wiggled, freeing herself from Mina's grip. Mina gasped, but Nukka landed lightly on the snow. She snatched up her harness and jumped up onto the sled, right next to Dad's feet.

"Okay, that's enough." Dad picked her up. Nukka tried to wiggle, but his hands were too big and strong. She wanted to mew her anger but didn't want to drop the harness still clamped between her teeth. Mom hurried over with the thermoses, which she handed to Mina before taking Nukka.

"You're staying with me, little one," she said, kissing the top of Nukka's head. "I think that's everything. Do you have the coordinates?"

Dad nodded. "Trooper Jack just sent them. The group lost track of him near Kilaun Pass. That's only thirty miles northwest. The path gets a little tricky, and visibility is pretty bad right now, but we've run this route before."

"Right." Mom's voice was light, but Nukka could hear the worry in it as she turned to Mina. "Be safe, both of you."

"Love you, Mom," Mina said, giving her a quick hug. "I'm going to check the harnesses one more time, Dad."

"Thanks, hon."

After kissing Dad on the cheek, Mom headed back inside. Nukka clung to her shoulder, looking back at the pack. At the front, she could see Niko watching her, the relief evident in her posture. Nukka felt another yowl of anger building inside her. Mina was young, but her mom and dad were letting her go on the rescue mission. They trusted her. Why couldn't Niko trust Nukka?

Inside, Mom closed the door against the chilly wind. Nukka could hear the pups wrestling and playing in the living room. Just as Mom set her on the floor, a loud crash sounded, and Mom sighed.

"What did you guys break now?" she called, heading out of the kitchen.

Nukka didn't hesitate. Still holding her harness,

she crept through the doggie door—and found herself face-to-face with Lola.

"What are you thinking?" Lola looked disapproving. "Do you really want them to strap you to a sled like a dog?"

"Yes!" Nukka felt defiant. "They're going to rescue a lost hiker, and I want to help!"

Lola flicked her ears. "It's not your place. What can you do that the dogs can't? You'll just get in the way!"

For a moment, Nukka felt defeated. Then she looked out into the yard, past the two straight lines of huskies attached to the sled, and into the woods. It was every bit as dark now as it had been when she and the pups had snuck out to run the obstacle course, plus it was snowing. *Visibility is pretty bad,* Dad had said.

And just like that, Nukka knew exactly how she could help.

"Mush!"

Dad's command was barely audible over the wind, but Nukka heard it. As the pack raced into the woods, Nukka lunged forward. Hissing, Lola leaped out of her way.

Nukka flew across the snow, running as fast as her paws would carry her. The pack was moving slowly, getting used to the weight of the sled, but she knew they'd pick up speed quickly. The trees loomed high overhead as Nukka followed the sled down the path, closing in fast.

The sled hit a bump that sent it a few inches in the air. Summoning all her strength, Nukka leaped as far as she could.

Yes! She landed on the footboard just as the sled hit the ground again. Nukka took a moment to steady herself, getting used to the feel of the sled bumping along against the ground. Dad stood right in front of her, his hands on the handlebars. Nukka peered at the rods that connected the bars to the front of the sled, where she knew Mina huddled in the little seat with the cargo basket.

What can I do that the dogs can't? Nukka thought as she took the first step onto one of the rods, carefully making her way to the cargo basket. *Sneak onto a sled, for one thing! Lola taught me how to be sneaky.* She reached the basket, slipped between the boots of an unsuspecting Mina, and climbed into one of the bags of supplies.

Nukka set her harness down and curled into a little ball to keep warm. Her heart pounded with excitement as the pack headed deep into the Alaskan wilderness.

Chapter Nineteen

Niko

As the trail turned steep and the pack headed up the side of the mountain, the snow began to fall faster. Niko raced fearlessly along the path, relishing the sounds of her pack behind her. Her paws remembered this route, even though they hadn't run it since last winter. It was tight in places, with the occasional steep drop-off on the left, so Niko made sure the pack hugged the right side of the trail. The one bonus of the freshly fallen snow was that it made for a smooth path—mostly. Niko still had to be careful of the occasional crack in really hard-packed snow.

She was more worried about the falling snow than the already-fallen snow. If it started coming down any harder, getting back home would be a lot more difficult.

The scent of the air changed slightly, a deeper, saltier smell that told Niko there was a steep drop ahead. She knew Suka sensed it, too, because Niko felt the lines connecting them shift as Suka moved to the left. Niko reached the turn, and Suka swung out as far as she could so that the rest of the pack—and Dad and Mina in the sled—made the turn safely.

The path continued straight on, and Niko picked up speed. She couldn't help remembering her dream of racing through a blinding blizzard only to discover the pack had vanished, and then that sound . . .

"Mew!"

It happened just as the sled hit a small bump. Niko's ears flattened, but she heard nothing except panting and the padding of paws. She must have imagined it.

She turned all her attention to her nose. Dad knew the general location of the last place the expedition group had seen the lost hiker, but he could have wandered even farther. Besides, there was almost no way anyone would be able to spot the hiker in all this snow. There was only one way to find him, and that was *smell*.

At last, Niko caught the scent of confusion and fear. The hiker wasn't on the path. He was somewhere in the woods on the left side of the trail—downhill.

Niko slowed her pace slightly, and a moment later, she heard Dad yell, "Whoa!" The pack came to a stop, and Niko turned to face the trees.

Suka was also sniffing the air, her pale eyes glinting. "I smell him, too."

The huskies peered into the trees, which were close together, the tops catching most of the falling snow. Dad hurried toward them, holding a giant flashlight. "He's down there, huh?"

Niko wagged her tail hard in response. She took another good long sniff, her mind mapping out a route down through the trees. The hiker wasn't too far away, but he wasn't moving—he was hurt, maybe even unconscious. They had to hurry.

"*Arf!*" Her bark was sharp and urgent, and Dad nodded.

"All right, Niko. Get us down there."

He headed back to the sled, and Niko heard him saying something to Mina. For a brief moment, Niko caught another scent, something familiar yet totally out of place. Then she felt the reins on her harness tighten, and Dad called, *"Mush!"* and they were off again.

Niko moved quickly but carefully, allowing her nose to find the safest path through the trees. The hiker's scent grew stronger—a spicy smell that was sort of similar to Dad's, but not exactly the same. The snow suddenly turned soft beneath Niko's paws, and with Suka's help, she guided the pack around a particularly thick trunk. Then she spotted him, leaning against a tree and shivering violently, and she slowed.

"Arf! Arf! Arf!"

The hiker looked up and saw them just as Dad called, "Whoa!" Niko came to a halt a few feet from the hiker. His furry hood was pulled down low, but Niko could see the relief in his eyes.

"Hey there!" Dad said lightly, grabbing a

flashlight and hurrying over to crouch next to the man. Niko watched as Dad spoke in a low voice to the hiker, who was gesturing to his foot. Dad patted the man on the shoulder, then got to his feet.

He unhooked Niko's leash from her harness, and she trotted back to the sled at his side, where Mina was waiting. Her cheeks were flushed with cold, but she gazed hopefully at her father.

"Is he okay?"

"His name's Ethan, and yes, he's in surprisingly good spirits, all things considered!" Dad rummaged around in the bag hanging from his handles and pulled out his two-way radio. "But his ankle is sprained, maybe broken. And we've got to get him out of this cold as soon as possible. Can you pull out the medical supplies while I let the troopers know his location?"

"Yeah!" Mina jumped up eagerly as Dad headed back over to the hiker, already speaking into his radio. Mina opened the large bag that had been sandwiched between her feet. Niko's fur rose as that scent hit her nose again, stronger than ever—familiar, but completely out of place. It smelled like ... But no, it couldn't be ...

"*Mew!*"

"Nukka!" Mina gasped as the kitten leaped out of the bag. Niko couldn't believe her eyes. She'd watched Mom carry Nukka back inside the house, where she'd be safe. How in the world had she ended up on the sled?

"Mina!" Dad called, and Mina blinked.

"Coming!" She grabbed the medical supply bag, then looked at Niko. "Watch her, okay? I'll be right back!"

As Mina hurried over to Dad and the hiker, Niko turned to Nukka. The kitten met her stern gaze without flinching.

"I wanted to help!" Nukka said.

Niko didn't respond. The atmosphere had changed, and she sensed something wrong. "Just follow me. Now."

She padded over to Dad and Mina, Nukka right on her heels. The pack fell still and silent, each husky staring in disbelief at the kitten. But Niko felt a sudden, sharp sense of urgency that wiped away her anger. She had time to let out one loud *"Arf!"* and shield Nukka with her paw before a great rustling noise sounded a few yards away, near the massive trunk she'd led the pack around just a few minutes ago. Niko remembered how soft the snow had felt there—because the tree was leaning, its roots ripped out of the ground. And now the top branches were weighed down with more snow than the tree could support.

CRASH!

Mina shrieked, Dad threw his arms around her, and everyone cowered as the massive tree fell, sending a shower of snow up in the air. Once it had settled, Dad looked around.

"Everyone all right?"

Niko glanced down at Nukka, who was trembling but okay. The rest of the pack stared at the fallen tree solemnly.

Suka met Niko's eyes. "There goes our path."

Dad remained calm, as always—it was one of

the things Niko loved best about him. "Mina, can you wrap Ethan's ankle?"

"Yes!" Mina set to work, carefully pulling off the hiker's boot. Niko watched as Dad walked a few feet away, speaking into his radio again. When Ethan let out a little laugh, Niko turned to see Nukka climbing onto his lap.

"You brought a kitten way out here?" His voice was hoarse and scratchy.

Mina smiled. "Not exactly. She's kind of a stowaway."

Ethan lifted a gloved hand to pat Nukka on the head, and she let out a soft purr. "Brave little cat," he murmured.

"Okay, here's the problem," said Dad on his return, kneeling down to help Mina secure the bandage wrap. "The snow started falling harder about ten minutes ago, and it's only going to get worse. The snowmobiles can't get all the way out here, but they can meet us at Creekwood Inn on the west side of the pass." Dad glanced over his shoulder at the fallen tree. "That means we've got to find another way back to the trail, off the path. Which is definitely more of a challenge for the pack."

His voice was light, but Niko heard the concern in his tone. Her nose could get them to the trail, but with the pack pulling three people now—one of them injured—things could get tricky. And the fact that a blizzard was starting wasn't going to make things any easier.

"I can help!" Nukka placed her tiny paw on Niko's, her eyes blazing with determination. "Please, let me help."

Niko almost protested. Then she paused. "How?"

"Cats have better nocturnal vision than dogs." Nukka lifted her head. "That's why I wasn't afraid of the tunnel in the obstacle course, even though Klondike was. I could see the end! I brought my harness. If both of us are at the head of the pack, we'll have my vision *and* your nose."

At the reminder of that night with the obstacle course, Niko felt another flicker of anger. But despite everything, she couldn't help but see the kitten's point. Plus, the trail wasn't far, and the pack would have to move extra slowly anyway, both because of the injured hiker and the blizzard.

If they were lucky, it just might work.

Chapter Twenty

NUKKA

Nukka tried her best not to shiver, in spite of the frigid air. She could feel the eyes of the rest of the pack on her, and she and Niko stared at each other. Finally, Niko dipped her head.

"Okay. Let's try it."

For a moment, Nukka thought for sure she'd misunderstood. Then she felt a surge of joy as Niko nodded toward the sled.

"Let's get your harness."

"Yes!" Nukka bounded across the snow, ignoring the stares of the other huskies. She leaped into the sled, found her harness, and jumped back out. When she reached Niko again, Mina caught sight of her and let out a little laugh.

"It's not really a good time to go on a walk, Nukka!"

Nukka set the harness down next to the hiker's leg, which Dad and Mina had nearly finished wrapping. How could she communicate her plan to them?

Then Niko picked up the harness and headed over to her spot in the pack. Ignoring Suka's look of disbelief, Niko dropped the harness and turned to face forward. Understanding dawned, and Nukka hurried over to stand at Niko's side, right by her harness. The message was clear, even to Dad and Mina: *Nukka will lead the pack, too.*

"Am I hallucinating, or does that kitten think it's a husky?" Ethan said, and his tone suggested he was only half kidding.

Dad shook his head and chuckled. "Trust me, you're not hallucinating. That happens to be a very special kitten."

Nukka sat nervously as Dad and Mina helped Ethan to his feet and led him to the sled. Once they had him safely buckled in, Dad came around to hook the lines back on to Niko's harness. Mina crouched down in front of Nukka, her brow furrowed.

"Dad, we're not actually going to let Nukka run with the pack, are we? What if she gets hurt?"

Dad sighed, and for a moment, Nukka thought her plan was doomed. Then she realized Dad was staring at Niko, not her. Slowly, Dad reached out and held the husky's face in his gloved hand, and Nukka had the feeling they were having a conversation neither she nor Mina could understand. Finally, Dad turned to Mina.

"If there's one thing I know about huskies, it's that they have great instincts. And Niko's instincts are exceptional. If she thinks having Nukka here will help us, I trust her."

Slowly, Mina's gaze moved from Dad to Nukka. The kitten waited anxiously, half expecting Mina to argue. But after a moment, Mina picked up the harness and strapped Nukka in.

"Be careful," she whispered.

Nukka sat up proudly. *I will.*

She glanced at Niko as Dad and Mina headed

back to the sled. The husky didn't meet her gaze, and Nukka knew she was still upset. But right now, Niko was focused on the mission. And Nukka was going to do everything she could to make sure they all got to the trail safely.

"Mush!"

The pack surged forward, and Nukka briefly felt the weight of the sled and its three riders tug hard at her harness. Behind them, Kodiak let out a deep *"Woof!"* and the line relaxed slightly. Nukka glanced questioningly at Niko as they slowly moved around the fallen tree.

"He's pulling more of the weight." Niko kept her eyes fixed ahead. "That's his job as wheel dog."

Nukka's nose twitched, and she led the pack around a clump of roots. They were climbing uphill, but it wasn't too steep. Before long, Nukka spotted the path ahead. *That wasn't too hard,* she thought.

And then she saw the snow.

The trees had been sheltering them from the

falling flakes, but out on the path, it was chaotic: what looked like billions and billions of snowflakes falling from the sky, the wind whipping them sideways and around in a complete frenzy.

Nukka glanced at Niko nervously.

"We're not going up there yet." Niko began to turn, and Nukka did as well. "Let's try getting through these woods first. Can you see?"

Nukka concentrated, staring as far ahead as she could. It was dark—super dark, even darker than when she and the pups had snuck out. But Nukka could see the outline of every tree. "I can," she said, and Niko picked up speed.

It was a slow trot for the huskies thanks to the roots and piles of snow and frost on the ground. But Nukka was thankful for the slow speed, because it was more than fast enough for her little legs. She guided them through a tight cluster of trees and around a mound of snow that had plummeted from the treetops, and spotted the edge of a dangerous crevasse just in time.

Suddenly, Nukka's harness pulled tight. She let

out a squeak and turned to Niko, who was also straining against her harness.

"Whoa!" Dad called, and the pack stopped pulling. Nukka heard Dad and Mina talking, and then the sound of footsteps. Moments later, Mina appeared in front of Nukka and Niko.

"You guys okay?" she asked, checking their harnesses. "The sled got caught on some brambles, but Dad's fixing it."

Niko nuzzled Mina's gloved hand. As Nukka caught her breath, she shivered. With all the pulling and running, she'd almost forgotten how cold it was out here.

Mina noticed the kitten trembling. She scooped her up and held her close, and for a moment, Nukka wanted to burrow herself in Mina's coat and hide in the sled for the rest of the ride.

Then Mina whispered, "You're doing a great job, Nukka. I'm so proud of you!"

And warmth rushed through Nukka from her ears to her toes.

"All clear!" Dad said, and Mina gave Nukka a

kiss before setting her down and hurrying back to the sled. Nukka stood as tall as she could, waiting for the command. *"Mush!"*

The pack leaped forward with renewed energy. At last, they reached a path through the trees, and Nukka saw that it was all clear ahead. Exhilarated, she picked up speed, and so did Niko. The rest of the pack followed, and soon they were all racing together through the snow.

Nukka spotted a tiny pinprick of light ahead on the right. It vanished, and for a second, she thought maybe she'd imagined it. Then she saw it again, and a third time, and a fourth time. Nukka bumped against Niko, urging her to shift to the right and head into the trees. Niko obliged, and a minute later, they both heard the rumble of snowmobile engines.

"This way!" Niko leaned harder to the right, and she and Nukka guided the pack uphill through the trees. A moment later, they burst onto the trail, where three snowmobiles waited outside a cozy-looking inn with a covered circular driveway.

Nukka could see the flashing lights of an ambulance and a van with FAIRBANKS DAILY NEWS painted on the side, along with about a dozen people all bundled in hats and coats, most of them holding up cameras and phones. When they caught sight of the huskies, a huge cheer erupted from the crowd. Nukka spotted the man with the hat, whom Mina had called Trooper Jack, hurrying toward them with a big grin.

Finally, the pack came to a halt on the covered driveway. Niko, Nukka, and the rest of the pack watched together as the paramedics, Dad, and Trooper Jack helped load Ethan onto the ambulance. After the ambulance drove off, several people swarmed around Dad and Mina, all calling out questions.

"Where exactly was the hiker?"

"How did you find him?"

"Were there any problems finding the trail in this blizzard?"

Nukka heard Dad answering a few of the questions, his arm around Mina as he spoke. A woman in a bright pink jacket and matching boots glanced over at the huskies, then did a double take.

"Is that a *kitten*?" she cried, aiming her phone at Nukka.

Suddenly, all eyes were on Nukka and the huskies.

"Her name is Nukka," Mina told everyone, her voice filled with pride. "She was a stray we rescued on the side of the road in September. And tonight, she helped us find our way back to the trail!"

"She and Niko here led the pack," Dad added, scratching Niko behind the ears.

The crowd surrounded them, taking pictures and videos and talking excitedly. Nukka was panting heavily, shivering and tired. But she'd never been happier.

They'd accomplished the rescue mission—all together, as a family.

❄ ❄ ❄

Over an hour later, Nukka awoke from a deep sleep. She was curled up inside Mina's thick coat, pressed against her belly. Nukka felt confused for a few seconds until she realized what had roused her from her nap.

The sled was slowing down. They were almost home!

A few minutes later, Mina stood up, arms wrapped around her coat to protect Nukka as she raced inside the house. Nukka could hear the other huskies as Dad removed their harnesses, and she felt a twinge of nerves. Was Niko still angry at her?

She heard Mom's voice as Mina unzipped her coat, and then Nukka was free. Mina held her out to Mom, who fixed the kitten with a mock-stern look as she took her in her arms.

"I was going out of my mind with worry, you naughty thing," Mom chided. "You have no idea how relieved I was when Dad called to tell me you were with them. What were you thinking, silly kitty?"

Nukka cuddled up to Mom, feeling guilty for scaring her by running away. Over Mom's shoulder, she saw Klondike, Miska, and Nanuk race into the kitchen. At the same moment, the back door opened and Dad and the other huskies piled inside the warm kitchen.

"She's not a silly kitty, Mom!" Mina said, her voice high with excitement. "You'll never believe this, but Nukka ran with the pack! And there were reporters at the inn where we met the ambulance and Trooper Jack, and they interviewed us, and Nukka might even be on the *news*!"

Mom's eyes widened, and she turned to Dad. "What?"

Dad laughed and shook his head. "It's true."

"Okay..." Mom said slowly. "Start with the part about Nukka running with the pack."

"A fallen tree blocked our path, so Nukka and Niko guided us to the trail where the snowmobiles were waiting," Dad explained. "I wouldn't have believed it myself if I hadn't seen it with my own eyes."

"She's a hero." Mina beamed at Nukka, and she felt a rush of pride and pleasure. Then Mom set her down on the kitchen floor, and Nukka realized several pairs of light blue eyes were fixed on her in disbelief.

"Well, I want to hear all about it," Mom said. "But the pups need some food, and you guys look like you need to warm up. How about I whip us all up some hot chocolate?"

"Yes, please!" Mina kissed Mom on the cheek, then sat down at the kitchen table and pulled out her phone. Dad pulled the vat of husky chow from the fridge, and Mom turned on the stove and began heating up a pot of milk. Immediately, the pups surrounded Nukka.

"Is it true? Did you really pull the sled?"

"That's amazing! How'd you do it?"

"Was it scary? Did you get hurt?"

Nukka sat perfectly still, her fur standing on end. The pups were all looking at her as if she was a hero, just like Mina said. But Nukka couldn't tell what Suka, Kodiak, and the rest of the pack were thinking. And she couldn't bring herself to meet Niko's gaze.

At last, Niko stepped forward. Her movements

were stiff, as if she wasn't happy at all. The pups immediately fell silent and backed away, tails between their legs. The rest of the pack cowered, too, and Nukka felt her ears flatten against her head. At the table, Mina lowered her phone and stared at the scene unfolding before her. Niko stopped in front of Nukka.

"You disobeyed my orders."

Nukka's heart sank. "I know, but—"

"*Everyone's* orders."

"I'm sorry, but—"

"You could have gotten yourself killed!"

"I thought—"

"But . . ." Niko leaned down until they were nose to nose. "You also saved us all."

Slowly, Nukka looked up. Niko's eyes were shining, and her tail began to wag. Soon, the rest of the pack were wagging their tails, too.

"Mom, Dad, look!" Mina exclaimed, holding her phone out to take a video as Klondike hopped on top of Nukka, then cuddled up against her, followed by Miska and Nanuk. Niko joined in, and so did

Suka and Kodiak and Sakari. And Nukka realized that it didn't matter if she was a kitten or a husky. All that mattered was that she felt happy in her own fur—and that her family accepted her.

As the whole pack enveloped her in a giant dog pile, Nukka finally felt like she was exactly where she belonged.

Chapter Twenty-One

Mina

@Gentrys6irl001: I can't believe I'm going to see you guys in
ONE WEEK!!!

@RachelLuvsHalo: I KNOW!! I might actually be more excited
about meeting you guys IRL than I am about actually seeing
ClockWork!!

@Lyricallee: I'M MORE EXCITED ABOUT CLOCKWORK

@Lyricallee: j/k ILU guys! 🖤

@MinasOriginalDesigns: One! Week! 😄

Mina did a little happy dance in her chair as she
typed. In the last six months, Mina's Original
Designs had *exploded*. She'd taken Faith and Fiona's
advice about making her Running Out of Goats
shirt a limited edition. Mina made twenty shirts

and charged twenty dollars for each of them. They'd sold out that weekend, and Mina had immediately gotten to work on her next limited edition design.

Word about her shirts had spread like wildfire on Instagram. ClockWork fans loved the detail Mina put into her designs, and they *really* loved the limited editions. Each time Mina posted a new one, the shirts would sell out within an hour. After two months, Mina had saved up enough money to buy a ticket to the ClockWork show in Seattle! Her parents were coming, too, and so were Emily, Faith, and Fiona (who, it turned out, were big ClockWork fans, even if they claimed not to be totally obsessed).

"Mina!" Dad called from down the hall. Next to Mina, Niko's head perked up. "Time to go!"

"Coming!"

Mina pocketed her phone, closed her laptop, and double-checked her appearance in the mirror. She was wearing her newest limited edition shirt, a round clock with only eleven numbers, inspired by ClockWork's latest single. She'd packed ten of them, along with twenty other shirts, in a box last night, wondering if she was being too optimistic.

"Okay, Niko," Mina said, picking up the box. "Ready for the first farmers' market of the season?"

Niko shot to her feet, tail wagging as she followed Mina down the hall.

Outside, Dad helped Mina load her box into the truck. "Did Mom leave already?" Mina asked.

Dad nodded. "There was no way to fit everyone in the truck."

Mina grinned. She couldn't wait for everyone at the market to meet the newest members of their family.

"Okay, everybody in!" Dad said, opening the door to the truck. Niko leaped in first, followed by Suka, then Kodiak. Mina giggled as Klondike—who already weighed almost as much as Kodiak now—clambered in after them and immediately got tangled in a seat belt.

"Are Miska and Nanuk with Mom?" Mina asked as Dad helped Klondike free himself from the seat belt.

"Yup."

"What about Nukka?"

Dad frowned, stepping away from the truck and squinting out over the yard. "She's here somewhere—oh, over by that tree. Is that Lola with her?"

Mina looked to see Nukka prowling along the edge of the woods, sniffing the ground intently, tail high in the air as she tracked a scent. She paused, then took a flying leap at a bush, and a frantic squirrel scurried out and tore up the nearest tree. Lola sat very still, watching the kitten closely. When Nukka turned to face her, she stood and stretched, taking her time. Then she began to sniff the ground, copying Nukka's movements almost exactly.

"What on earth are they doing?" Dad wondered aloud.

Mina grinned. "I think Nukka is teaching Lola how to track like a husky. Mrs. Ferguson told me Lola has been getting better at catching mice."

"Is that so?" Dad laughed, shaking his head with a smile. "Nukka! Let's go!"

The kitten's head shot up, and she flew across

the yard. Mina watched as Nukka launched herself into the truck, scrambling into the back seat with the huskies. Nukka had grown a lot over the spring, but she still looked like a tiny kitten next to Klondike. That didn't stop her from wrestling with her brother over a piece of old rope the entire drive to the farmers' market.

"Whoa," Dad said when they pulled into the parking lot. "I don't think I've ever seen it this busy!"

Mina had to agree. It was a chilly but sunny day, and it seemed like everyone in Fairbanks had decided to visit the market. But there were lots of tourists, too—Mina could tell by their brand-new ski jackets and boots.

Dad and Mina carried their supplies to their tent, followed by the huskies and Nukka. A crowd of people were already there, all cooing over Sakari's new litter—five fuzzy, wriggling pups, only two months old.

Mina could hear Mom's voice over the giggles and "aww"s of the crowd. "This one is Eska, and that one over there is Takanni. Oh, here's the rest of the pack!" Mom waved as Dad and Mina approached, and a few people glanced back at them.

Then a girl a few years older than Mina gasped. "Oh my gosh, is that Nukka the Husky Cat?"

Mina looked over at Nukka, who was still trying to tug the rope clamped firmly between Klondike's teeth. Before she knew what was happening, dozens of people swarmed around Nukka and the huskies, most of them snapping photos on their phones.

"This kitten is, like, an Instagram *star*," Mina overheard the girl saying loudly to her friend. "She totally acts like a husky!"

Mina and Dad exchanged a grin as they each began unpacking their boxes. After they'd successfully rescued Ethan, the story had gone viral. *Kitten leads sled dogs and lost hiker to safety!* Mina had created another Instagram account: @NukkatheHuskyCat. Within weeks it had ten times as many followers as @MinasOriginalDesigns. But Mina didn't mind. Especially considering Dad had ended up booking excursions every week from December through

March. It seemed like everyone who visited Fairbanks wanted to ride in a sled pulled by a pack of adorable huskies and one very unique cat.

"Hey there, boss!"

Mina turned quickly at the sound of her best friend's voice. Emily stood there, grinning as she watched everyone laugh at Nukka and Klondike's antics.

"Hi!" Mina said. "Are Faith and Fiona here yet?"

"I think they're at Faith's mom's booth." As she spoke, Emily opened the box of T-shirts. "How many boxes did you bring?"

"Just this one," Mina replied.

"Seriously?"

Mina and Emily looked up to find Faith and Fiona standing behind them, wearing twin expressions of disbelief.

"You should've brought more!" Fiona told Mina. "You're going to sell out of these before lunch!"

Mina laughed. "I doubt it. Last time I tried to sell these at the market, I had literally zero customers, remember?"

"Yeah, but... wait." Faith's eyes widened. "You mean you haven't checked Instagram?"

"I did earlier," Mina said, confused. "Why?"

"No, it was just, like, fifteen minutes ago." Faith grinned. "You're going to *freak. Out.*"

Fiona whipped out her phone. "Hang on, I'll show you!"

Mina glanced at Emily, but she looked as mystified as Mina felt. Then Fiona held out her phone. When she saw the screen, Mina thought she might faint.

"Oh my god. Oh my god. *Oh my god.*"

It was a photo.

Of Gentry.

Wearing Mina's limited edition goat shirt!

Emily let out a shriek, and Fiona and Faith were both talking at once, but Mina barely heard a word. She was reading the post beneath the picture.

@TheOneAndOnlyGentry: thx so much to superfan @GentrysGirl1001 for sending me this AWESOME SHIRT by

@MinasOriginalDesigns!!! Now I just need one for Ozzy the Goat! 😂 #clockworkfansarethebest

Mina couldn't process it. Gentry. From ClockWork. Was wearing. Her shirt. Slowly, Mina pulled out her own phone for the first time since getting into the truck. He'd posted fifteen minutes ago, like Faith said. But already, Mina had *over a hundred* new notifications! The first one was from Hallie.

@GentrysGirl1001: SURPRISE!!!! 😊 😊 😊 😊 😊 😊 😊

"He tagged you," Emily said, grabbing Faith's phone. "Mina, Gentry *tagged* you!"

"You're practically besties now," Faith said with a giggle.

Fiona gasped. "Maybe we can meet him in Seattle!"

"Yeah!" Faith cried. "Mina, you could make a shirt for Ozzy and we could give it to Gentry after the concert!"

Mina pressed her lips together tightly. She was afraid that if she tried to speak, she might scream with joy instead.

Emily caught sight of her expression and giggled. "I think she's in shock."

"Hey, are these ClockWork shirts?" The girl who'd recognized Nukka peered into the box and pulled out one of the new limited editions. "Wow, I love this one! How much?"

"Thirty dollars," Fiona said, and Faith and Emily hurriedly started unpacking the shirts. Mina suddenly realized her eyes had filled with tears. A cold nose pressed into her hand, and she looked down to find Niko gazing up at her in concern.

"Don't worry, they're happy tears," Mina said, kneeling down to hug the husky. Over by the pups, Nukka's head swiveled in their direction. The kitten sprinted over, hopping into Mina's lap and purring loudly.

Mina gazed around the tent. Mom was introducing the pups to a group of squealing kids, while Dad helped a couple sign up for an excursion. As

Fiona handed the girl some change for her purchase, Emily and Faith finished setting up the display.

"You know what, guys?" Mina said softly, looking from Niko to Nukka. "I think this summer's going to be a *lot* better than last year."

Niko nuzzled Mina's hand in agreement, and Nukka squirmed happily in her lap.

"Mew!"

Acknowledgments

Huge thanks to my editor, Orlando Dos Reis, for digging into the first draft of this story and helping me find its heart, and to my agent, Sarah Davies, whose nose can't be beat when it comes to tracking down deals. I'd also like to thank everyone at Scholastic, including Amanda Maciel, Caroline Flanagan, Kerianne Okie Steinberg, Priscilla Eakeley, Claire Flanagan, and Lori Lewis—the best literary groomers out there.

Special thanks to the wonderful people who work at the Dallas Animal Services & Adoption Center and Cane Rosso Rescue, who helped me find my wonderful foster doggo, Jake, while I was drafting this book, and to anyone and everyone who volunteers at shelters and rescue organizations for pets. Heroes, all of you. Adopt, don't shop!

About the Author

Michelle Schusterman is the author of over a dozen books for kids and teens, including *Spell & Spindle*, *Olive and the Backstage Ghost*, and the series The Kat Sinclair Files and I Heart Band. She coauthored the YA novel *The Pros of Cons* with Alison Cherry and Lindsay Ribar, and coauthored the Secrets of Topsea series under the name M. Shelley Coats. She currently resides in Dallas with her husband and two food monsters disguised as Labs.